WHEN WE ARE

Anthology of Award-winning Short Stories

ISBN-13: 978-0-9851833-0-1
ISBN-10: 0-9851833-0-6

DEDICATION

This anthology is dedicated to those who
know when we are

To the authors featured in this book: Scribes Valley thanks you for
your time, patience, trust, and talent.

.

CONTENTS

WHEN WE ARE
A Foreword by David L. Repsher, editor

I love old pictures of people (as opposed to pictures of old people). There's something about looking at someone from a by-gone era. Maybe it's the look in their eyes, maybe it's their smile— or lack of a smile, maybe it's the way they are posed.... I don't know. It's hard to put into words.

Whenever I look at an old picture of people I realize it shows so much more than just people. It is a microcosm of the time the picture was taken, a museum display of their era, a depiction of their *when*.

My modern eyes stare into their ancient eyes and something seems to pass between us, not only from the picture to me, but from their time to mine. It's amazing to think that, at the time the picture was taken, *they* had the modern eyes, *they* were up-to-date.

In this age of digital pictures, I wonder what our legacy will be. A hundred years from now, will people stare at our pictures on computer screens and wonder how we lived? I think they will. I guess it's just human nature to wonder about things like that.

The next time you take a picture of yourself or others appreciate what you are doing. Realize that pictures are so much more than just pixels arranged into something coherent. They not only show who we are or the current fashions, they show *when we are*.

FIRST PLACE

THE BLAZER WITH TWO RIGHT SLEEVES
©2012 by Dan Sullivan

The O'Neil twins were late for everything—weddings, graduations, Thanksgiving dinners, Friday Night Poker at the Elks Lodge. On each occasion, the middle-aged bachelors would arrive scruffy and out of humor, to offer their separate but identical apologies. "I'm sorry I'm late, but you know how my brother is."

Procrastination was a life-long character defect of Brendan and Rory O'Neil. Their dear, departed mother, in tears, had often tossed up her hands and guessed that it probably started even before they were born with the two of them rough-housing inside of her, losing track of time, and finally arriving three weeks after their due date. She had always been at a loss on how to fix it. Sweet talk, the "cold-shoulder" treatment, prayer, fasting, devil's food cake—nothing worked, and to her dying day, Mary Margaret O'Neil considered herself a bit of a failure that her dear, sweet boys could be so mean as to let her leg of lamb get cold each and every Sunday.

Catholic school didn't fare any better than Mrs. O'Neil. Sister Arcangela, Principal of Nativity School, was fond of announcing upon the twins' unswervingly late arrival, "Ah, here they are!" And with that, the stately Franciscan—also now long departed—would launch into a lecture on the downside of "tardiness"—a lesson which always ended with the admonition, "Brendan and Rory O'Neil, you two will be late for your own funerals."

Actually, she wasn't off by much.

Brendan wasn't late for his own funeral that day, but he was about a half an hour behind schedule—give or take a few minutes—to welcome the mourners at his twin brother Rory's wake.

It just didn't seem real. None of it did. The call from the emergency room had come three nights earlier. By the time Brendan arrived they had done all they could, but Rory was gone. Robotically, Brendan answered their questions. "Yes, heart disease ran in the family.", "No. He wasn't married. Single all his life.", "Yes, we'll want McReady's to handle the arrangements." As he was leaving, a nurse handed him a grocery bag that held his brother's blazer, his necktie, and a watch, an hour behind the correct time.

"...actually, I don't believe in Daylight Savings Time."

"Rory, have you lost your mind?"

"No, having to constantly reset your watch—springing forward, falling back...that's insane."

"No, what's crazy, Rory, is you always making me late..."

Brendan resolved that he would get things done and be on time for the viewing. He would get a haircut, he would have his suit pressed, and he would go to an early AA meeting so he could have a word or two with Rory before the mourners arrived. But he broke every one of the promises he had made to himself: he got neither his hair cut nor his suit pressed and went instead to an AA meeting at noon, which left him with no time to spare. Then there was midday traffic, and when he finally got to McReady's Funeral Home, the tiny parking lot was already jammed. Only a prayer to his sainted mother helped him find a spot a few blocks away.

Then it came out of nowhere—the urge to have "a cold one," not just any beer, but that lovely one he had had a lifetime before. It was July 1960, a year before they buried their father. *Dan O'Neil and Sons* had been laying sod at a country club. Brendan was working his way up an incline, thrusting his spade into the yellow lawn, jacking up the sod, pitching slabs into the barrow, staying barely ahead of the muffled thumping and tamping that grew louder behind him.

When the job was done, the O'Neils sat in the cab of their truck and drank beer so cold that their throats burned. That was what he wanted now, what he once would have died for, but Brendan knew that he had dallied too long with the memory so he reminded himself about the folly of half-measures and recited the Serenity Prayer. The craving began to dull, and, at last, rumpled, out of breath, and angry, he reached the front porch of McReady's.

AA had taught him that it wasn't the thirst that drove him to drink. Beneath the urge for drinking and carousing was procrastination, and beneath the foot-dragging were more than a little vanity and a lot of anger. And Brendan's anger and irritability had found, by high school at least—probably earlier—an available target in his twin brother, Rory, and a workable medium: disputes over facts all clouded by aging memories and an obstinate refusal to consult verifiable sources.

"Brendan, for your information, Don Larsen pitched his perfect game in the 1956 World Series."

"Wrong again, Rory. It was the 1955 series because we were still living in Brightwood. End of discussion!"

Cherished nieces and nephews had tried to intervene. At Christmas and on birthdays, they would bear neatly wrapped peace offerings in the form of books and software. Encyclopedias, almanacs, dictionaries, compendiums were all presented in the vain attempt to keep pace with the latest disagreement. Over the course of years, the neglected presents began to overrun the bachelors' apartment.

"O.K., knucklehead. I'll bet you twenty bucks. Mickey Mantle was a rookie in 1952."

"Wrong us usual, Brendan. It was 1951, DiMaggio's last year with the Yankees."

Brendan took a deep breath and then removed his glasses before going inside McReady's. You never knew when Janet or Susan Whelan from the old neighborhood just might show up even though he hadn't seen either one in forty years.

The black and pink shapes of the mourners against the sidewalls of the parlor floated past Brendan. At the casket, he felt as if he had stepped into a cave of flowers, and the place where he stood was oddly lighted—vague and out of focus yet somehow far too bright. It was like the time that they had been summoned on stage to sing "Wild Colonial Boy" at Nativity's St. Patrick's Day assembly. He was aware of an audience full of mourners and that he and Rory were now center-stage, with him playing the mourner and Rory acting dead.

Brendan made the Sign of the Cross and kissed his thumb before he knelt at the casket. "Our Father..."

It took a little time to work up to it, but finally Brendan squinted at Rory. Brendan saw his own face, still and powdery, his own head resting on a white satin pillow in the casket. He kept waiting to see if Rory would flinch or blink or move a finger signaling that it had all been a mistake, that it was time to call the whole thing off, that they hadn't properly rehearsed any of this. But there was no sign, just Rory asleep in the casket, his waxy hands folded just above his waist and fingering a rosary.

"Fifty dollars says it was Goldwater who ran against Johnson in the 'sixty-four election."

"That's the easiest fifty I ever made, Rory. If you had half a brain, you'd be dangerous. It was none other than Richard Milhous Nixon."

"...forgive us our trespasses as we forgive those...."

"And by the way, genius, Sammy Baugh led the league in punting and interceptions as well as passing in 1942."

It was no use continuing. Even in death, Rory bothered Brendan so much and then made him feel guilty about it to boot that he couldn't even say a prayer for his own departed, aggravating brother. But the failed prayer did give Brendan a chance to slip his glasses on and inspect the corpse. After all, he and his nephews were paying handsomely for the arrangements.

Ye gods!

Danny McReady, owner and head mortician, whose thirst was legendary, must have been deep in his cups when he did Rory. There was no other explanation. It was either that or Danny had turned one of his interns loose on Rory: he looked horrible! Just an hour into the wake, give or take a few minutes, and already the powder had begun to cake at the corners of Rory's mouth. Then there was Rory's expression, the one they would remember him by, the one Rory would carry to the seat of judgment.

Brendan said that he expected his twin brother to look "dignified. Dignified and serene." McReady's Funeral Home, however, had rendered Rory neither *dignified* nor *serene*: somebody had fiddled with his mouth—setting it in a kind of devilish grin for all eternity. Then the *pièce de résistance*: the presentation of Rory.

Rory was laid out in his navy-blue blazer—the one with two right sleeves that he had bought over the Internet for $24.99—plus shipping and handling. The blazer, the dance lessons, his bad dye-job, the gym membership...each was emblematic of Rory's desperation to find someone to share his final years. Hope for that ended three nights earlier during a Texas Two-Step lesson when Rory crashed into folding chairs along the wall of the studio, dragging his instructor to the floor. Probably nobody at the wake but Brendan would notice the stubborn eddies of fabric on what was supposed to be the left sleeve of Rory's jacket. Still...

"Brendan, come here. Look at this." On the monitor in Rory's room was a cartoon figure with a magnifying glass examining a suit. A caption trumpeted: Even the pickiest shoppers have a hard time finding anything wrong with our clothes. Nearly perfect attire for a song. Men's Blazers starting at $24.99 plus shipping and handling!

"Read between the lines, Rory—'have trouble finding fault with,' 'nearly perfect'—doesn't that tell you something? Doesn't

that say to you that they're really selling you a piece of...?"

Within a week, Rory's nearly perfect, navy blue blazer arrived.

"You have got to be kidding me. The thing has two right sleeves, Rory. You're not going to wear that thing out in public, are you?"

"Of course I am. I'll just be wearing it at night."

By the time Brendan had blessed himself and stood, his Aunt Annie, the O'Neil twins' eighty-year-old godmother, who never could keep the two of them straight, was waiting to extend her hand and condolences to Brendan. Brendan kissed her forehead and squeezed her skinny hand, which felt loose and delicate like warm crepe.

"Rory, I know how much you loved your brother, but Brendan's in a far better place. And I have to say he looks just wonderful. Danny did such a wonderful job. So calm. So..."

"Dignified?"

"Exactly!"

Deep in the summer of 1970. "The O'Neil Boys Back from Nam!" Straightaway, both landed jobs at a nursery: Rory on the early shift, Brendan on the late. A Friday. Brendan left work early and when he got home, they were dancing in the living room. The German nanny from down the street had her arms around Rory's neck and chided him playfully in a deep, husky voice as they stopped.

"Vat's wrong?"

"Nothing."

"Vat's wrong, baby?"

"Nothing."

Brendan's early arrival had had a chilling effect on Rory and his chance for romance. It seemed like minutes of silence, then she muttered and noisily collected her things before marching toward the front door. Rory followed, imploring. Over her shoulder, she called back, "Vogeddit, buddy." Rory at the front door and Brendan from a living room window watched her as she clomped down the front steps and out of their life, in a yellow sundress and clogs.

"I guess you screwed up your chances with her, Rory," Brendan said brightly with a can of beer in his hand.

"Not really, Brendan, I told her I was you."

With one hand cupping her elbow and the other holding her upper arm, Brendan guided his aging aunt onto the kneeler and stood awkwardly behind her in the odd light near the casket. When Aunt Annie had finished mourning the wrong godson, Brendan helped her up, and they turned away.

The parlor was now packed. Besides the O'Neils, almost every other family from their old neighborhood was there. After about an hour or so of greeting and reacquainting, a voice intoned, "We are here this evening to offer the Sacred Mysteries of the Most Holy Rosary for the repose of the soul of Rory O'Neil and for the needs of his loved ones." Then there was a grand, extended rush as the able-bodied mourners knelt. Brendan stole a look at Rory who still held his expression of malevolent humor about the whole affair.

Late summer just before the start of seventh grade. They had just turned twelve. Brendan was tired of always being with Rory, dressing like Rory, and especially sharing birthdays with Rory. Brendan wanted just to run away and stop being Rory's twin. After practicing the speech several times to himself, he announced to Rory in the alley behind their house that they couldn't be friends any more, that they were getting too old to be playing together, and that some of the guys even said they were "weird," always with each other. Brendan declared that they both had to be on their own and play sports and find girlfriends, now that they were almost in junior high school. Brendan remembered looking at his other self: Rory lost and stunned at first. Then Rory's face shattered. At the far end of the alley, a black man in a red flannel shirt swung an ax and buried it in a log, but the sound didn't reach them until he had raised the ax once more above his head. Rory's face was twisted in rage and pain. He balled his fists and was crying. "I hate you, Brendan, you stupid moron." Rory ran down the alley toward the man who again silently buried his ax in the log.

Brendan knew that if you looked long enough and hard enough at something lifeless it would almost seem to move. That had been the case when Brendan could have sworn that their father moved two or three times during his wake. Brendan had been looking at the corners of Rory's eyes since they started the prayers to see if there would be the slightest signal that it was all a mistake. Still Rory lay motionless as if petitioning for his own cause with a rosary in his waxy hands.

"Holy Mary, Mother of God...."

The rhythm of the mourners' prayers made it sound, when Brendan closed his eyes, like the rush and retreat of the sea.

"Pray for us sinners, now and at the hour of our death...."

Rory and Brendan had taken their assigned places in the den for the family Rosary that night. It was 1952, and they were praying for world peace and an end to communism. Rory and Brendan nudged each other during the first five minutes or so, but it was Brendan who finally got exiled to the hallway, and afterwards, their father sentenced Brendan to bed, even though it was only 7:30. How delicious it was being alone in their room under the cool sheets—away from Rory, alone with the light of early evening on the bedroom walls. He heard Rory and their little sister chasing each other back and forth across the yard...back and forth.

Someone had blown his cover and Stalin's thugs were pounding up the stairs to the roof. Any moment they would get him, and the Commies had so many unspeakable ways to make a man talk. It was either death by torture—or leaping to the sidewalk below. But that was suicide and a mortal sin. When Brendan woke up, it was dark, and he was tangled in his sheets at the foot of his bed. Rory was asleep, but Brendan shook him awake and asked, "Rory, can I please sleep with you? I'm having a bad dream."

Brendan climbed into Rory's bed, and they held each other. Rory patted Brendan's shoulder and muttered sleepily, "Don't worry, it's just a dream." The eight-year-old twins and best friends huddled fast asleep. A few more years would pass before Brendan put an end to play in the alley....

Then for the first time since Rory's heart attack, Brendan cried. His grief sounded foolish and reluctant, like a sneeze among strangers. He pictured the twelve-year-old Rory, his face twisted in pain and rage, balling his fists then running away down the alley. Then another image of Rory came to mind. It was just before he left for his dance lesson on the night he died. Standing in front of the mirror, adjusting his tie, Rory looked...*My God! Lonely and afraid! And just when did his shoulders get so thin?* The sneeze came again and again, and then Brendan couldn't hear any more the rush and retreat of the mourners in prayer.

He and Rory had been together since the first division of cells. They had huddled and tumbled together as they grew inside their mother, kicking and touching and grappling. Three weeks after their due date, they arrived: Brendan was delivered first, then Rory. But now...

Rory, what am I supposed to do now, you idiot?

Several elderly mourners were straggling through the concluding devotions. Then there was an extended rush as the mourners stood and by degrees the parlor emptied as Brendan thanked each one for coming. No sign of the Whelan sisters.

Finally, Brendan was by himself with his back to the casket. He decided against going back. He had already said his goodbye, and it was slippery enough for him tonight. He'd probably have to read the AA Big Book into the early hours and keep saying the Serenity Prayer to make it through.

It was ten o'clock when he got home. He called his AA sponsor but got his answering machine. Still, just making the call had steadied Brendan enough to face the apartment alone.

For the past week or so, with making arrangements for Rory's funeral, notifying Rory's creditors, and getting to meetings, he hadn't even checked his computer. He turned it on, and there were fifteen unread messages waiting for him. Most he deleted, but then he came across one from *r.oneil@epa.us.gov.*

Brendan said the Serenity Prayer and opened the message Rory had sent from his office the day he died.

The attack on Pearl Harbor was December 8, 1941, jackass!

Easter Monday, the first day of their weeklong vacation from Nativity School. Everything was yellow and lavender and jungle green in the April sunlight. Sister Kieran had assigned no homework, and they were free. Brendan chased Rory across a field. 'You're it!' Then away from Rory with his brother in pursuit in the sweet April breeze. Before you knew it, it would be Daylight Savings Time, then the school picnic, and dismissal at last for the whole summer. The nine-year olds stopped running and lay in the grass that had become tall and thick while they were asleep the night before. Rory draped his arm around Brendan; Brendan did the same to Rory. They squinted at the crystal sky. They were copies of each other in every way—the same brown, wavy hair, the same slanted blue eyes.

"Do you think Debbie Reynolds is pretty?"

"She's O.K."

"How about the Spanish lady in High Noon*?"*

"Oo la la."

They laughed and punched each other, then jumped up and raced home.

Brendan picked up a framed family photo next to his computer. He touched the spot where Rory stood among the O'Neils. Rory suddenly became small and began to float behind what seemed like smeared glass. Then he flamed out from the others and grew closer, and a feeling like whiskey bloomed inside Brendan. But it wasn't whiskey: Rory was reaching out to him from an Easter Monday far away...and beneath the anger was a feeling Brendan had no name for, but it came on at times like twilight, in the alley behind their home, and it never failed to fill his eyes. It had something to do with the losses in his life and the time he put an end to play with Rory, more than forty years before.

Brendan closed his eyes and whispered in his heart where he knew Rory could hear him, "I hate to disappoint you, Einstein, but it was December 7, 1942."

About the author:

Imagination transformed early experiences of mine and helped create "The Blazer with Two Right Sleeves." Now, that piece has a life of its own. And while the story is just that—a story— the shadow of my brother Richard crosses it and has given it life. I am honored that Richard and I will be part of Scribes Valley's latest short fiction anthology.

SECOND PLACE

THE VISIT
©2012 by Ronna L. Edelstein

The red Cyclops-like eye of the elevator glares at Vera. No matter how many times she punches it with her fist, it neither blinks nor vanishes. Using words that would no longer shock her once demure and genteel mother, Vera swears at the smirking button, but only the ghosts of past visitors and residents hear her profanity. She wishes she had the power of Odysseus to either make the light fade—a sign that the elevator has arrived—or, even more to her liking, to see the light turn a brighter emergency red, a sign that the elevator has broken, and she will be able to postpone her dreaded journey. Again and again, she pounds her index finger against the light, hoping that her attack will crack the eye's protective glass covering. But the red eye continues to stare at her, mocking her attempts to control it.

In the two years she has faced that red-eyed monster, Vera has never once succeeded in conquering it. On those days when she and Dad anxiously want to reach what they call the penthouse, the red button ignores her angry, impatient finger and takes its time in bringing the elevator to them. When she and Dad wish they could escape the inevitable visit, the red button blinks almost before she presses it.

Today, Vera waits by herself. A bronchial-like cough, runny

nose, and pounding headache have kept Dad at home. He fears he will infect his already frail wife should he visit, but he does not want a day to pass without someone seeing Ma. Even though Ma no longer communicates with them, Dad and Vera still sit with her while she eats lunch, and then they spend a few hours either watching her sleep or taking their own naps. When Dad walks with Ma up and down the hallway, Vera washes Ma's feces-stained and urine-scented underwear and other clothing. She re-arranges the already neat drawers, and she dusts that nightstand that has not had time to gather more dust since her last visit.

Despite Vera's reluctance to make this visit on her own, Vera cannot say no to the father who stood by her side when the prom limousines arrived at everyone's house but hers, when the rice of her wedding turned into the glassy shards of divorce, when surgeons cut into her breasts for possible malignancies, and when more shadows than sunlight marked her life. That is why she finds herself waiting impatiently for the elevator to come so that her visit with Ma—the woman who always disappeared when Vera most needed her, intruded when Vera most longed for solitude, and criticized when Vera most craved acceptance—can start and, more importantly, end.

Vera also seethes with anger—at Dad for getting sick, at Ma for getting Alzheimer's and ending up in the nursing home, and at the elevator that refuses to come. The stench of the parked cars seeping through the glass door that separates the garage from the lower lobby burns her eyes; Vera fears she will choke on the fumes and die in this lobby with its dirty tiled floor and cracking cement walls. And Ma will not even know that Vera tried to visit her but asphyxiated in the process.

Vera spends the next five minutes counting the tiles on the floor but loses her place after reaching number fifty-eight. Remembering how she used to lie on the soft backyard grass and, while Ma hung wet clothes on the line, search for images in the clouds, she now tries to decipher faces and forms in the lines marring the once white walls; all she sees, however, are Ma's veins—collapsed veins that refuse to accept the intravenous needle with its nutrients, bruised veins that have experienced too much pain, thick veins that stand out like coiled rope against papery skin.

Again, Vera punches Cyclops, still hoping to smash the button and cause a flow of red tears to drip from Cyclops' eye. She imagines the tears floating across the floor, rising until they reach her ankles and knees and hips. She will drown in the red tears of Cyclops—but at least she will not have to enter that elevator that will take her to Ma.

Closing her eyes, Vera rocks back and forth as if in a trance. She tries to empty her mind of what awaits her, but a grunting noise—the sound of exhausted, aged joints still trying to do the job of a younger person—jolts her back to reality. Cyclops' red eye fades to black as the ancient elevator door creaks open.

As always, Vera stands in the front of the small metal cage. Her claustrophobia makes her hope that no other passengers will join her for the short ride to the real lobby of the facility, but the elevator again jolts to a stop and opens its gaping metal jaws to welcome three more passengers. Vera does not budge from her front-and-center spot; she claims squatter's rights. Two of the new arrivals quietly go to the back of the elevator, but the third—a bird-like woman with blue hair and matching blue veins on her twig-like arms—stares at Vera with wounded eyes. The eyes let Vera know that this ancient crone is not a visitor, but rather a resident of this demonic place. All the residents have eyes dimmed by defeat and hopelessness.

Vera surreptitiously studies the other two passengers—a middle-aged man dressed in a dapper hat and overcoat, and a middle-aged woman wrapped in dark fur. At first, she defines them as siblings because both share the same full lips, elongated nose, and eyes the color of mud, but when the man reaches for the woman's hand and, in knightly fashion, kisses it, she sees the rings that identify them as husband and wife. Although Vera can only guess as to whom they are visiting, she feels certain that they are virgin visitors due to the frightened look emanating from their eyes. She does not know them, but she hopes that the person they have come to see resides on one of the first four floors, the home to wheelchairs, walkers, canes, and people who still retain a semblance of normalcy. Only the fifth floor—the penthouses where Ma and others like her reside—evokes images of snake pits, cuckoo nests, and hell.

The elevator stops on another level, stretching its mouth to make room for a female patient and her rotund private aide. The aide, oblivious to Vera's claustrophobia, pushes Vera into the back corner of the elevator. When one more stop brings two more passengers into the shrinking space, Vera starts to gasp for air; she clutches the metal railing of the elevator, hoping that this thin, tarnished bar will prevent her from collapsing onto the carpeted floor stained with mud and drool, despair and frustration.

An animated conversation develops between the resident and her aide as the elevator struggles to reach the lobby. Apparently, the two women had combined a trip to the doctor with a stop at a nearby ice cream parlor. Although both laugh as they debate the merits of mint chocolate chip over banana and chocolate swirl, Vera blinks rapidly in a futile attempt to hold back tears. The last outing with Ma, which took place about two weeks earlier, had been a disaster from start to finish. Ma's refusal to get out of her wheelchair forced Vera to lift Ma into the car—an effort that left Vera with a sprained back, despite Ma's skeletal frame. Once at the ophthalmologist's office, Vera had to monitor Ma like a kindergarten teacher on a playground with a recalcitrant six-year-old: "Don't touch that instrument, Ma", "Ma, you can't put those pads in your pocket", "No, Ma, it's not snowing in the office, but you are littering the floor with pieces of dirty Kleenex."

When the elevator comes to a stop, Vera pushes aside courtesy and the other passengers and rushes to her freedom. She finally stands in the real lobby, although Vera finds nothing real about the huge hall with its faux fireplace, copies of Renoirs and Monets, and aides who hide their disgust of the setting and its population behind pretend smiles. As always, Vera heads to the reception desk, signs in, and asks the lady with the outdated bouffant blonde hair and heavily made-up eyes who sits behind the desk to press the magic button that will allow the elevator to go to the locked-down top floor.

Vera again stands in the elevator. Her only companion is the trepidation she feels as the cage transports her closer and closer to Ma. Visiting Ma often makes Vera feel as if she has entered a carnival's house of mirrors; she is never sure which image of Ma she will see or how Ma will perceiver her. Sometimes an ancient woman, a twin to Norman Bates' mother rotting in the cellar of the Bates house, awaits Vera, while other times Vera detects glimmers of Ma's former feistiness in her eyes. Ma usually recognizes Vera as someone integral to her life, but that person could be a sister, a made-up niece, one of her two granddaughters, or a childhood friend who now only exists as a fading black and white photograph in the family album.

With a sigh, the elevator releases Vera into an inferno that not even Dante had the courage to explore. Vera first walks by the lounge, a large room with a television that always blasts game shows or soap operas to its indifferent audience of shadows: the professor who no longer knows how to read or write, the great grandmother who thinks she is a young girl and keeps calling for her mother, the husband and wife who find comfort in others but not in each other. Vera passes the room of the newest inmate who loves to press the fire alarm and see the brigade of men in red uniforms converge on the floor. This woman does not realize that even the strongest and most powerful fire hoses cannot douse the flames of lost memory that have seared her and the other residents.

Vera holds her breath as she approaches the dining hall whose tables and floor look like a Jackson Pollock painting of splotches of red spaghetti sauce, dots of white milk, circles of brown gravy, mounds of yellow salad dressing, and curlicues of blue and green medicines. She hears one man moaning over and over again,

"Please give me food. Please give me food," even though she knows his untouched lunch sits in front of him. Another resident, a round-faced woman with piercing black eyes, uses her spoon as a drumstick; she pounds and pounds on the table, creating a noisy tattoo that accelerates the pounding in Vera's head. No one speaks to Vera, although a few residents study her as though she reminds them of someone who wanders in and out of their confused minds.

One aide nods at Vera, first asking about Dad and then sending best wishes for Dad's speedy recovery. She tells Vera what Vera already knows: "Your mother chose to stay in her room for lunch today." Ma, the woman who spent hours cutting out coupons to save nickels and dimes at the grocery store and who fought the Black Friday mob of shoppers to get a bargain, would be horrified to know that every meal she ate in her room added another charge to the already exorbitant cost for her room and board. Dad and Vera had tried to explain this financial reality to Ma, but Ma had long left the world of the rational.

Vera finds Ma lying in bed, her eyes blinking as if trying to focus on some distant memory. She tells Ma that she has arrived and that Dad, Ma's husband of sixty-five years, has not come due to illness, but Ma remains still until Vera removes a package of chips and cookies from her purse. For a woman who embraced an anorexic approach to eating and who judged Vera by her body weight not her character, Ma has developed a craving for salt and chocolate that both baffles and bothers Vera, a somewhat thin sixty-year-old woman who fears that should she eat even a crumb of these sweet treats, she will look like Jack Sprat's wife who could eat no lean and lose any chance of winning Ma's approval.

Ma devours the treat and, realizing that no more goodies await her, closes her eyes. Vera takes her usual position in the torn leather chair across from Ma's bed. She takes out her book, but finds herself too distracted to read. Instead, Vera stares at Ma and wonders how this diminished woman can be the formidable foe who once dominated her life. Although Ma rarely speaks, Vera can still hear her shrill voice criticizing Vera for the A-minus that should have been an A, for the slumped shoulders that not only accentuated Vera's ape-like posture but also defined Ma as a bad parent, for all the times that Vera failed to live up to impossible expectations. Vera hears Ma tell her that she will never win a beauty contest, that she needs to emphasize academics because she will never soar socially, and that this too will pass. Venomous words spew forth from the mother who no longer exists, creating such rage in Vera that she pushes herself off the chair, grabs her book and coat and purse, and heads toward the door.

Across the hall lies the Invisible Man, the label Vera attached to this resident when he moved in several months earlier. Vera has never seen his face because the man never leaves his bed, at least not during Vera's hours of visitation. Instead, like a corpse, he lies with a white sheet covering his face. Only the slight up-and-down motion of the sheet lets Vera know Invisible Man still lives. No pictures decorate the walls of his room, and no knick-knacks clutter his dresser. His room even lacks a clock to mark the passing of time. Everyone on this floor—the visitors no longer recognized by family members, the family members no longer recognized by visitors, and the residents who no longer see themselves as viable human beings—is invisible, Vera decides. That insight weighs Vera with a sadness that causes her to postpone her exit from—and abandonment of—Ma.

Vera takes one more glance at the shrouded Invisible Man and heads back into Ma's room. Opening Ma's closet, she runs her hands over the t-shirts that Ma wears, the blouses with bows that Ma wore all her life but now refuses to put on, and the floral sweatpants that Vera recently bought to bring some color to Ma's wardrobe. When Vera discovers a few shirts and skirts that do not belong to Ma, she does not worry. The residents have the tendency to shop—to wheel or wobble into another person's room and grab a blouse or family picture or handful of candy from that person's closet, shelf, or drawer. Since the residents have no sense of ownership, they do not know when something is missing from their room. Ma, who still has the mobility of a walker, embraces shopping; this woman who threw out the family photo album because "the pictures were old" now seems intent upon crowding her room with pictures of other people and their families.

Even now, three years after Dad had hesitantly told her about the murdered album, Vera feels acid burning her throat and stomach. That album had held Vera's past. She would sit on the floor, hold the album on her lap, and create happily-ever-after fairy tales involving the little boys in knickers, the little girls in straw bonnets, the women in long dresses, and the men with waxed moustaches. These stories allowed Vera to tolerate her real life—the one with the mother who rarely smiled, who feared happiness like others feared disease or failure, and who, like in a game of *Mother, May I* would take one step forward and three steps backward in her relationship with her daughter.

The cremated album, a victim of the building's incinerator and Ma's lack of caring, still pains Vera, but, since Ma's illness, Vera has learned that Ma cannot be held culpable for her acts. Ma is a child who does not understand what she does, why she does it, or the consequences of her actions. Sometimes, like a puppet gone wild, Ma shakes her hands at Vera or, if Vera is in close range, hits her on her shoulders or chest. Other times, Ma rubs her hands together like Lady Macbeth, but Ma seems to be searching for something from the past, not trying to rid herself of signs of past guilt.

A familiar odor causes Vera to leave the closet and her memories for the diaper and bed Ma has just dirtied. Dad usually handles this aspect of Ma's care, but Dad is home sick. Vera knows she should call for an aide—someone who, by not knowing the "before Ma", may cause the "after Ma" less embarrassment at the situation. Yet, Vera opts to lift Ma from the bed and help her to the bathroom, convinced that she, the daughter, will treat her once proud mother with respect, unlike the impersonal and not-so-gentle aide.

Oblivious to Vera's internal debate, Ma stands passively in the bathroom as Vera cleans her and places a new diaper on her. She sits quietly as Vera rubs lotion over her flaking legs and then combs her thinning gray hair. Vera wonders whether or not Ma remembers those summer days when Ma poured a solution of baby oil and iodine over her body and baked in the sun, while Vera gave her a pedicure with a Q-tip and water and then rubbed Ma's legs with cream. Maybe Ma does recall the hours she and Vera spent in the basement—Ma ironing shirts and tablecloths, and Vera diapering, dressing, and playing with her family of dolls. Vera, whose maternal instinct did not transfer from her dolls to her two children, is surprised that these simple motherly acts for Ma bring her solace. For the first time in their lives, she can support Ma without worrying about a non-verbal backlash or a curt "I can do it myself" retort.

Vera gently helps Ma sit on the leather chair while she replaces the soiled sheets with new ones. Then, she leads Ma back to bed and, before she can change her mind, also crawls into the narrow twin bed with her. She and Ma lie together like two matching spoons sharing a drawer. Vera wraps her arms around Ma and patterns her breathing after the slow, regular beats that emanate from Ma's heart. Speaking in a voice that can barely be heard over the ticking of the clock, Vera whispers to Ma about how much Dad misses her, about how her grandchildren are planning to fly in and visit her, and about the latest play she has seen and book she has read. Vera's softly spoken words take Ma to those evenings when Ma hosted her Mah-jongg club. Ma always baked a lemon JELL-O pie for the women and one smaller version of the pie just for Vera. One special night she even let Vera play a round of Mah-jongg with the women.

Although Vera cannot see Ma's face, she imagines that Ma smiles with pride when Vera praises the meat loaf and roasted potatoes Ma prepared every year for the school picnic at the community amusement park. Vera expects no answer, but she still asks Ma if she remembers driving her to and from school when even one dark cloud appeared in the sky, and if she remembers the countless hours she spent teaching Vera to parallel park so Vera could pass her driver's test on the first try.

Ma, whose voice has weakened from lack of use, listens in silence as Vera continues her storytelling of a time so long ago that sometimes Vera fears she is making it all up. Vera laughs as she reminisces about the family vacation to New York City decades earlier and how Ma confused the steps to the subway with those to the ladies' restroom. She tells Ma that she still cannot take a bath without seeing Ma, sitting cross-legged on the bathroom mat, watching her splash in the bubbles while teaching Vera her ABCs and 123s. Vera describes how the aroma of egg salad sandwiches always awakens within her a deep-rooted hunger for those carefree summer days before Ma began working. Ma would load the car with Vera and her older brother, some neighborhood kids, and a basket of food, and then took everyone to the suburban pool for the afternoon. The best part of the day was sitting next to Ma on the worn bedspread and eating the delicious concoction of white bread, mayo, and chopped eggs.

As Vera pauses for a minute, allowing both she and Ma to reflect upon those memories that she has excavated from the rubble of anger and time, Vera suddenly feels Ma rubbing her arms with her gnarled, arthritic fingers. The motion soothes Vera like the "secretary's lunch" of soup and a sandwich Ma always prepared for her on a blustery school day or the quilt she would tuck under her chin before turning on the night light and closing Vera's bedroom door. Then, in a voice softened by Ma's tender touch, Vera speaks again. She transports Ma to their day-after-Thanksgiving shopping trips to downtown department stores where they fought the bargain-hunting mob to find shirts for Dad. She takes Ma to the specialty diner where, for a short time, Ma ignored cholesterol and calories, and joined Vera in a lunch of cheeseburgers, fries, and thick chocolate shakes.

The heat in the room, the darkness created from the closed blinds, and the comfort from lying next to Ma cause Vera to fall asleep. For the forty minutes of her nap, Vera's graying hair, wrinkles, and aches and pains of the tarnished golden years become pigtails and bangs that never lay straight due to a stubborn cowlick, a nose pink and peeling from the sun, and a wanderlust that refuses to be satiated. Vera and Ma, each licking a swirled chocolate-and-vanilla ice cream cone, dance in the waves along the shore in Miami Beach. They carefully blend chocolate chips into the cookie dough before baking one huge cookie as a treat for Vera's brother. They sit opposite each other at the dining room table and, while devouring a mini Thanksgiving dinner, discuss everything from the Depression that destroyed Ma's teaching dreams to the college degree that granted Vera a life in the classroom.

Ma's stretching causes Vera to awaken. At first, Vera remains the little girl of her dreams; she thinks she has the flu and that Ma has lain beside her in case Vera needs a sip of Ginger Ale or a cool washcloth for her forehead. A groan from Ma, however, reminds Vera that *she* is now the caregiver and that Ma lives in a place that Vera cannot visit.

Reluctantly and sadly, the aging Vera releases her arms from around Ma; the coldness of the separation inundates her, mocking the warmth of the embrace. Vera starts to get up, but Ma rolls over, reaches for her, and caresses her face with her hands. With an almost ethereal gentleness, Ma kisses Vera's forehead. Then, Ma turns Vera's head so that her lips press against Vera's ear. In a raspy whisper, Ma says, "I love you."

Hearing Ma say those words awakens in Vera that special spot from which emanates all the colors and music and aromas and sights—all the magic of memories both real and imagined—that make life worth living. Vera again sits in the chair by Ma's bed, oblivious to the noises outside the room: the serene voice of one aide trying to calm an agitated resident, the frustrated voice of another aide as the new patient apparently finds a way to reach the fire alarm and set it off. Vera barely notices the vinegary stench of urine that never totally goes away or the cave-like darkness that dominates Ma's room since open blinds disturb Ma. She sits in the chair until Ma falls asleep, and then she quietly gets up and leaves.

Rather than engage in another confrontation with Cyclops, Vera opts to take the steps from the top floor to the garage. The long walk down will give her the chance to reflect upon her visit and Ma's parting words; it will postpone her inevitable return to a world of schedules and obligations and rare minutes of contemplation. Vera knows that Dad will ask her about Ma and the visit, but she decides not to tell him the details just yet; she wants to keep what happened a secret that only she and Ma share. Vera will probably just smile at Dad, kiss him on the forehead, press her lips against his left ear—the one that still functions with the help of a hearing aid—and whisper that she loves him.

Vera will not add, "Just like Ma loves me." She does not want the words, like the petals of a dandelion, to blow away and disintegrate into wisps of wishful thinking. Instead, she will take the words to bed with her, carry them with her when she again confronts Cyclops, and rely upon them when they become lost in the muddled maze of Ma's mind. She will make the words a part of every visit with whatever version of Ma awaits her.

About the Author:

I am a teacher and a lifelong student, a daughter and a parent, a caregiver to my 95-year-old father and a recipient of others' care. I am a dreamer and a doer, an optimist and a realist, a lover of M&Ms and daily workouts on the elliptical. I am a thinker and a writer.

As a part-time faculty member of the University of Pittsburgh's English Department, I work as a consultant at the school's Writing Center. I also teach Freshman Programs, a course that introduces students to the University and the city. My work, both fiction and nonfiction, has appeared in *New Slang, A New Literary Voice by the Women and Girls of Pittsburgh* (online); *Quality Women's Fiction*; *Ghoti Online Literary Magazine*; *First Line Anthology*; *The Road to Elsewhere* (Scribes Valley Publishing); *Welcome to Elsewhere* (Scribes Valley Publishing); *Visiting Elsewhere* (Scribes Valley Publishing); *SLAB: Sound and Literary Artbook*;

Pulse: Voices from the Heart of Medicine (online magazine); *AARP Bulletin* (online and print); *Healthy Roots* (Forbes Health Foundation and Hospice); *The Jet Fuel Review* (Lewis University's online literary journal); and the *Pittsburgh Post-Gazette*.

THIRD PLACE

THE BREATHING KIND
©2012 by Michelle Wotowiec

It's cold. Seven degrees cold. I feel the sting of Northeast Ohio in my lungs so I hold my breath. It hurts as I finally exhale and again inhale. I hold the icy air in the back of my throat, trying to warm it. The headlights and car horns on the street behind me try to grab my attention with no prevail. I look at my feet and think my skin looks blue. It might be the airport's outdoor lighting. Or maybe it is the moon's glow mixed with that of the headlights. It is possible, though, that my blood isn't circulating.

I look at Mom to my right without turning my head. She is cold too, I can tell. But she has more meat on her bones. A lot more. One hundred and fifty pounds more. Her skin rolls off her bones in layers and right now I'm jealous. If only her bones are cold, her skin is a coat. A thick insulated coat.

In Aruba, no one believed she was my mother. "You are travelling partners?" the tan-skinned men would ask in a heavy accent. "Oh no, she is my daughter," Mom would respond, proud. At least I think she is proud. Back in high school, I probably would have been embarrassed to be claimed by her. Not anymore, though. On the plane when she had to ask for a seatbelt extension, I wasn't embarrassed. Instead, I was worried. She is almost fifty and only gets heavier with the years. Two hundred and fifty pounds now she claims, but by looking at her I'd guess she is pushing closer to three hundred.

I held my breath longer than I should this time. I'm coughing.

"Are you okay?" I hear a man's voice to my left ask.

I continue to cough and nod my head.

"Are you sure?" He is wearing a long, black pea coat. His hair is dark and cut short. He's attractive. Like me, he appears to be in his mid-twenties.

Again, I nod, trying to hold in a cough.

"Cold night, huh?"

I don't say anything in response. I'm too cold. Too cold to talk. Years ago, I might have tried to be friendlier. Sweeter, cuter. I grew out of all of that, though. Not that I'm not friendly; I am, normally. I love talking to people. I love meeting new people. I love hearing travel stories (although I imagine this man is on his way home from a business trip and the story would probably be pretty boring). I've come to be more selective, though. If we were in the lobby waiting for a chauffeur to pick us up, I'd definitely smile and tell him all about Mom's and my weeklong getaway. I'd tell him about the pirate ship and the great people I met down there. I'd tell him about my first experience snorkeling and how small I felt in the blue water. I'd describe how my feet floated with the flippers, and how at the time, in the water, I imagined that is how it would have felt to be on the moon. The moon and the water, I thought, might have similar laws of gravity. Then he'd probably correct me. I'd smile anyway and keep giving him all of the intimate details of my trip. Nothing personal, though. Intimate, sure, but not personal.

I wouldn't tell him about how concerned I was with Mom's health all week. How she struggled for breath after twenty steps through the airport. How she had to take two breaks when walking up the hill to the hotel. I wouldn't mimic the scratchy sound her chest made while she slept at night. I wouldn't draw him a picture of the way her torso was similar to that of a whale on the queen-sized bed and her arms like little fins. I wouldn't tell him how sometimes, when I let myself think it, I'd see how she was becoming less and less humanlike in her figure and how the whole world seemed to know it would only be so long before she would explode. She would get so fat that she would explode.

I chose not to say anything to this man. Like I said, I have become selective with age. It is too cold to talk. I appreciate his effort, but it's not going to happen right now. I am concentrating on not breathing.

"Where is the bus, right?" he asks.

I don't look at him. I will admit that the thought has crossed my mind as well. Every fifty minutes the shuttle to Park Place is supposed to come. Or was it every fifteen minutes? I don't know. But I know it feels like an hour. That probably isn't right, though. The cold has a way of manipulating time.

"I know, this is absolutely ridiculous," Mom's voice responds from my other side.

No, Mom. Don't fuel the fire.

Luckily, he doesn't say anything. Maybe, like me, he realizes complaining isn't going to get us anywhere. If anything, it is going to make it feel worse. Longer. I prefer to hold my breath.

One one thousand, two one thousand, three one thousand, four one thousand, five one thousand, six one thousand...

One of my first memories takes place on some beach on the east coast. I am with Mom and we are laughing. She shows me a starfish she found on the beach. She flips him over and shows me his pulsating censor. *He's breathing—this creature is breathing,* Mom says. She looks thin in her red bathing suit. She pulls her long hair back behind her shoulders and we are laughing as we make our way into the water to throw him back in.

When I was a teenager, we were close. Very close. I told her everything. I told her about my boyfriends. I told her when I first had sex. I told her when I continued to have sex. I guess I didn't have anything too out of the ordinary to talk to her about (we all have sex, right?), but whatever I did have to say, I said. We spent lots of time together. She shuttled me to basketball practice, to the skating rink, to friends' places. Every Saturday we did breakfast and a movie in Medina. The year after I graduated, though, things went sour. She started crying all of the time. She started talking more than listening (looking back now, I'm not sure how much listening I really did growing up). She started talking about premonitions in her dreams and witchcraft (I know, that was out of left field).

At first, I blamed it on the drinking. Whenever she drank liquor, she'd open up. She would scream and cry and claim the government was spying on her through the television set. She would get so drunk she would fall. I remember the ground shaking as her body hit the dewy grass and I wondered how I would ever be able to get her back to her feet. I remember wondering how many other people at that exact moment had the same problem to worry about: how do I lift this two-hundred-and-fifty-pound drunken, crying woman to her feet? I thought it was just the drinking so I hated her for it. If she would stop drinking, she would stop being crazy. *So stop drinking.*

She did. We sat on the couch together on a Thursday afternoon. I know it was a Thursday because Thursdays were the days I got out of class early. Too early to meet up with anyone for late night coffee or dinner. I had no choice but to come home. So we sat on the couch, her hands were in her oversized lap and my body was pushed back. I was crying. Crying hard. Snot-running-down-my-face-and-through-my-fingers hard.

"You've got to stop drinking," I managed to spit out.

"I know."

"You know?"

"Yes."

And she did stop. Things didn't get better, though. Like I said, I thought it was the drinking, but it wasn't. The drinking was more like the door. The hinge of the door, maybe. The liquor let her thoughts slip through her lips. She quit talking about it. She stopped yelling about the television, but she continued to unplug it every chance she got. She put a lock on her bedroom door where she kept her crystal ball, pendulums, and Tarot cards.

One of my most recent trips home involved me tripping over a large bucket in the second-floor hallway. I couldn't see anything. The light had burnt out. I felt my way through the blackness, pulling the bucket behind me. Water, there was water splashing over the sides as I pulled. Heavy. It was so heavy. Not wanting to make any more of a mess, I gave up pulling it into the light of the bedroom. I dug through some kitchen drawers and found one of Dad's flashlights. The walk up the stairs should have taken longer. Shining the light into the bucket, I saw that it was full of urine and feces.

"Jesus Christ," the man in the pea coat says. He sounds mean. Like me, I think, he has grown to be more selective. I'm sure he wouldn't normally get so nasty in front of me and Mom. It was the cold. I'll blame the cold.

"You're sure it was Park Place?" Mom asks me after she blows her breath on her hands.

"Yes, Mom." I try my hardest not to sound annoyed as I let out the mouthful of breath I was trying to hold into the cold air. I vividly remember parking the car and saying *Park Place, like Monopoly* and she was sure it would be easy to remember.

"Where the fuck is this *goddamn* bus?"

For the first time, I turn my head to get a good look at the man. He seems less attractive. Thinner. Taller. His coat has water stains, his boots are covered in salt. His cheeks are dark red. I want him to see my glare, but he doesn't. I'm no longer on his radar.

This time, Mom doesn't say anything. I think she feels his fire burning, too, and knows better than to feed it.

I didn't really know what to expect for our weeklong getaway. Even when we were close, back when I was a teenager, we never spent this much time together. Seven days and seven nights. That's a long time. The past few years she had gone on cruises with her mother the first week of January. This year she wanted to do something different. She decided on the resort route and, because

I had just turned twenty-five at the end of December, she wanted me to come with her.

I wanted a break. I was working too much. Christmas time is always busy in the restaurant industry and my calves hurt. Classes didn't start back up until the second week of January. It was more about getting a break than going to a paradise with my mentally unstable mother. I figured I could handle it.

The first day we checked in, ate dinner, and drank piña coladas at the pier. I took pictures and we smiled and posed. The weather was beautiful and we were feeling good. The next night we took a party bus and shook maracas in the moonlight. We danced the *merengue* with some other tourists and sang Spanish songs we didn't know. The next day we took a boat and she watched as I snorkeled in the clear blue water. She laughed when the Aruban workers told me I was beautiful and had a great smile. Then we went off road in a jeep with two lesbians. They drove and we sat in the backseat, enjoying the ride. We lay around the pool, she read and I wrote. We drank more piña coladas. Then we went on a pirate ship and she watched as I swung from a rope and fell into the water.

"Holy shit, it's about fucking time," the man in the pea coat says as we see the Park Place bus pulling up. "I can't believe they would let you ladies stand in the cold this long. You have got to be freezing," he says to me, placing his hand on my shoulder. His touch feels crippling. I want to tell him to take his weight off of me. He is only making me colder.

I don't respond to him. I am not even sure he really expects a response. He is so furious, I'm sure I am being used more as evidence for his anger than as a confidant. Mom exhales, a sound of her relief. I'm shaking. Shivering. Teeth chattering. *Shivering is your body's way of keeping warm,* I hear an Aruban man explain to me on one of the snorkeling boats. I was cold in my bikini without a towel. It was raining and windy. He came over and rubbed his hands on my shoulders before giving me the worldly knowledge.

"Park Place?" the driver, a man of about my age, asks the three of us as he steps out and grabs our suitcases. Mine first, then Mom's.

"I will carry my own stuff, *thanks*," the pea coat man snaps when the driver tries to grab his luggage.

We follow the man up the stairs. He takes the front seat, placing his luggage on his lap. The bus driver comes back in and closes the door. He reminds me of a grown-up version of a guy I smoked pot with once. Andy, I think was the guy's name. He had the same boxy face and broad shoulders. Andy was wearing a Slipknot hoodie. I can definitely picture this driver in a Slipknot hoodie. He has the same eyes. Kind eyes, actually. The kind of guy who had a nice aura to him. Even if we were kids getting stoned, breaking the rules, etcetera, etcetera, I somehow knew he had good things ahead for him. And he did. Like me, he grew out of all that and went off to law school. At least that is what I heard.

"Are we going to move?" pea coat guy snaps. Even his voice is annoying me now.

"We have to wait for the other bus to get here before I can leave."

"Excuse me?"

"We have to wait for the other bus to get here before I can leave." The bus driver sounds passive. I know how hard it must be.

As a server, I deal with this shit all the time. Assholes with attitudes.

I look at Mom. She is looking at the floor.

"That's funny. The other bus didn't wait for *you* to get here," pea coat says. I see him fumbling his hand in his pocket and think he might have a gun.

"There was a little bit of confusion."

I move closer to Mom. I place my hand on hers and she squeezes my fingers.

"Oh, *obviously*." He looks out the window and pulls his hand out of his pocket, empty. "What's your name?"

No. Don't tell him.

"Mike."

"Okay, *Mike,* I tell you what. You move this bus right fucking now and get me to my car or I will get your ass fired. How's that sound?"

"I can't—"

"Move the fucking bus!"

I look at Mom. She is still looking at the floor.

"I can't—"

"Goddamn it, MOVE THE BUS!" Pea coat is standing up now. I am starting to sweat.

Mike moves the bus.

Mom behaved herself in Aruba, more or less. The past few years, she has been more vocal again. No alcohol needed. She printed up pens and business cards back in July: *Mary Godles, your psychic detective.* Dad laughs. Well, he laughs whenever I bring it up. It isn't a vicious laugh. It is an uncomfortable, avoid-the-situation laugh. I never have the heart to push it far. Sometimes I feel bad that I jumped ship. I wonder what he thinks about when he is alone in the living room, knowing she is at the top of the stairs crying to a crystal ball.

While in Aruba we met a lady who worked for a company that Grandpa's company used to sell a product to. We were meeting her for drinks later that night. I was washing my face in the sink when Mom said: "Shells, not to sound paranoid, but if she starts asking you anything personal about the business—or about the customers we sell to—don't tell her anything."

The only other incident happened the fourth day in Aruba. We were sitting on the pier drinking piña coladas when she said "Did you see the footprints in the bathtub?"

I hadn't. "Footprints?"

"Yeah, there were footprints in the bathtub."

"Oh God, I hope there isn't an animal in the room." I imagined an iguana slipping through the sheets of the bed and crawling around the bathroom.

"No, it wasn't animal footprints. I had to scrub them off when I was bathing."

"Weird."

"I think I know what it was."

"What?"

"You know how I use that Johnson's Baby Powder for my belly?"

"Yeah..."

"Well, I spilled some on the floor. I think the cleaning lady saw it and thought it was cocaine."

"What?"

"She thought it was cocaine so she called the authorities to come check it out."

"No."

"That is where the footprints came from."

"Mike, don't expect to have your job tomorrow," pea coat man snarls as he exits the bus. I imagine him falling on the ice before he gets to his car, but he doesn't. I guess he didn't have a gun. Maybe it was the cold making me overreact.

"Where are you parked, ladies?" Mike asks.

"I'm sorry for him, Mike," Mom says from beside me. She stands up and finds a place closer to the front. "That man had no right to talk to you that way."

"Thank you, but don't worry about it. I deal with people like him all the time."

I feel the burn in my lungs and hold my breath as I step off the bus towards the Pacifica. We wave bye to Mike and I think I hear Mom tell him to keep his head up.

"You driving?" Mom calls to me, as I am a few steps ahead. I nod and fiddle with the unlock button. I climb in and close my door, exhaling the warm breath out of my mouth.

"It's so cold!" I finally say. This is the first time I have let myself say it aloud. Saying it somehow makes it more real. Sort of like when I get sick. If I admit I am sick aloud, I feel so much sicker. It is better to suck it up and keep it in.

The windshield is buried in snow. The entire SUV is buried in snow which has accumulated throughout the week. Only hours ago I was in ninety degree Aruba, wearing sunglasses and shorts.

I'm only ten minutes from home. Warm bed, heated blanket. Ten minutes—if I had not had to drive with Mom to the airport. Instead, I am forty-five minutes from Mom's and another forty-five minutes from home.

"Oh shit." Mom says with guilt in her voice.

I don't want to ask what. I am afraid of what I will say. I am cold. I am like the dickhead pea coat man. Sadly, I see the similarities. It is the cold. I am sure pea coat man isn't always such a royal asshole. No one is always that mean. I am guessing once he gets home, has a good night's sleep under his own warm heated blanket, he will feel horrible for how he treated Mike. No one can be such an asshole. He'll be embarrassed, even.

I have a little more control than the man. Sure, I choose my battles—I wasn't up for talking in the tundra while we waited for the bus—but I would never yell at the bus driver like he did. No way. I deal with way too many assholes at work. Hungry people, like cold people, have very short fuses. So no, I wouldn't ever yell at Mike the way he did, but I might get smart with Mom.

I was driving us home from a Green Day concert back in 2005. We were here in Cleveland. Mom was wasted—crying in the backseat. She'd already pissed her pants and was trying to open the door to jump onto the highway.

"Let me out!" she yelled through snot and sobs. "Let me the *fuck* out!"

I didn't respond.

"I know they're paying you! I know you are trying to drive me crazy! *You're* doing this to me!" She stopped, panted, and began again, "My parents, my goddamn parents, they're poisoning me. They are putting rat poison in my food."

By this time, I'd learned the value of silence. Thirty-five more minutes and I'd be home free.

I shake off this memory, this feeling, as quickly as it slipped in.

"Oh shit," Mom says again.

"What?" I, surprisingly, don't sound annoyed.

"I don't have a scraper."

"What?"

"I don't have a snow scraper."

I look at the windshield and I can't see through the snow. Oh shit. I wish I would have thought to grab socks when I packed for Aruba. If I had thought to pack socks, I would not be wearing red sequined flats with bare skin. My feet wouldn't already be sitting in the standing water of my flats.

"I'll use my arm." She opens her door and I think I hear the ground rumble beneath her feet as she jumps out of the SUV. I am too cold to move and only watch as she starts wiping snow off the windshield with the sleeve of her coat. She comes in after fifteen seconds and closes the door hard. She brings her hands up to her mouth and exhales. "It's so cold." Exhale. "Give me just a second." Her face is bright red.

"Don't we have anything we can use?" I turn around and look at the backseat of the SUV. One thing Mom and I don't have in common is cleanliness. If we were in my Focus, we would find all sorts of stuff to use: old notepads, books, shoe boxes, dirty towels, a kitchen chair. Her SUV, though, as expected, is spotless. I try to think. Neither of us have gloves. We weren't ready for this. I open my purse. Nothing.

I open the door and lean through without stepping out into the snow. I wipe as much snow off as possible. My skin stings. My fingers are wet. Blue, I'm sure my fingers are blue. I come back in.

"Shit!" I let out involuntarily.

"I know! It is so cold!"

"Maybe if I rev the engine, it will help warm it up faster."

"Yes!"

I remember mowing the lawn for her last summer. It was going to be a surprise. Dad said she was having a hard time again, so I thought I'd come over while she was at work and mow the lawn. She'd be happy. Well, I flooded the mower by revving. Too much gas into the engine.

We wait. Breathing breath clouds into the air in front of us. We take turns getting out and wiping the snow. Under the snow, though, is ice. A layer of ice an inch thick.

I look at the clock: 12:39. My coat is drenched. I'm never going to get home.

"Let's breathe on the windshield!" she suggests. Breathe on the windshield? She scoots up and begins exhaling as close as she can to the windshield. I join her. I join her and we both blow every bit of air we have onto the windshield.

We're laughing.

About the author:

Besides the obvious writing and reading, Michelle loves cats, vegetarian food, and horror movies. She is proud to be published by Scribes Valley Publishing three years in a row. Her work can also be found in the literary magazine Prime Mincer 1.2. Her writing has been chosen as a finalist by Glimmer Train on three occasions as well as by Writer's Digest. She has received her English MA from Cleveland State and looks forward to spending her free time writing fiction. She thanks you for reading her work.

THE GHOST OF EARL WARREN
©2012 by Vanessa Orlando

Late on a Sunday afternoon in late Spring, no one is on First Street Northeast. Not one tourist. Not one bureaucrat. Not one cop. Not one living soul. So I sit on a cement wall in front of the U.S. Supreme Court, my back to the U.S. Capitol, and watch the ghost of Archibald MacLeish walk down the street and shake hands with the ghost of Thomas Jefferson, who is always coming around this way to visit his books. They stop when they see me, tip their hats or raise their canes, and walk on, embarrassed that there is still someone who can see them.

Last Sunday, the ghost of Earl Warren came out of the Court, stood at the top of those massive marble steps, and shook his head, but I couldn't tell if he was amazed or disgusted. I was barely a teenager when he died, so to me he was always an old man. An icon, born old. On the steps of the Court some 36 years later, he looked no younger and moved no faster, so by the time he turned to go back inside the bronze doors had shut and locked him out. He seemed confused, but he patted the door as if it were an old friend, assuring it that he would wait for it to open and let him back in.

When he looked out away from the Court, his face broke into a smile and he waved with his arm up strong and straight. He seemed less frail than he had a moment before, less frail than all the pictures I remember seeing of him in the history books. He skipped down each of those forty-four marble steps and enthusiastically shook hands with the ghost of Plessy, backslapped the ghost of Miranda and Gideon, gave a warm hug to the ghosts of Brown and Marshall. Only after those reunions did he see me.

"Hello," he said, slowly. Squinting.

"Mr. Chief Justice," I said, "it is an honor. How have you been?"

"I am well, thank you. Oh, I am sorry, dear. I don't remember all of you. You are ...?"

I leaned in and whispered, "...of this world."

His expression contorted as if he had just missed a golf putt he should have made. "It's getting harder and harder to tell. May I?"

I nodded as he sat next to me on the concrete wall.

"So, Judge," I asked. "What do you think?" I waved my hand toward the panoramic view of the Capitol behind us, its new multi-billion-dollar Visitor Center, the empty street.

"Everything's locked now, isn't it?" he said. "Locked down and walled up tight. You can't go anywhere around town now without a belt buckle setting off an alarm, can you? "

"I guess not," I smiled. "The world is a lot more dangerous now than it was when you were here."

He turned to face me. "No," he said sternly. "It was always dangerous. You could get murdered then as easy as now. My father was murdered. The President of the United States was murdered. The world, this country—life everywhere has always been dangerous. Always."

"True," I said, "but..."

"Never mind. Never mind," he waved his hand dismissively. "Do you have a key?" he asked, pointing to the front door of the Court. "To get back in? Everything I am is in there."

I laughed. "Well, everything *I* am is in this bag and there's no key to any door in it. Besides, you can't go in that entrance anymore, Judge. You can only come out. You have to enter through the side or the back or somewhere."

His eyes widened and he stared at the six-ton doors. "You're not allowed to enter the United States Supreme Court through its front doors?"

"Afraid not," I said. "Security concerns. I think they're locking up the justice to keep it safe from the rest of us."

"They've locked up the Supreme Court," he said matter-of-factly. "They've locked up even that."

"No, Judge. Just the front doors," I said. "You can still go in, you just have to go through a new entrance that's bomb-proofed, or something, I think."

He shook his head. "They wanted to hang me," he said. "People who said they believed in God and righteousness and the Constitution advocated hanging me, the Chief Justice of the United States. They made bumper stickers calling for my impeachment. Remember? *Impeach Earl Warren. Impeach Earl Warren.* Everywhere you looked. They wanted to send me *back* to Russia, because of course I had to be a Communist for all this propaganda about equal justice and such. No one ever suggested we lock the doors to protect me or my Court. Not once. Not ever."

"Maybe they should have."

"No, no." He shook his head more vigorously. "No!"

Chief Warren stood up abruptly and walked up the forty-four marble steps with determination and a straight back. He stopped to read the inscription above the bronze—*Equal Justice Under the Law*—and found the doors still locked.

"For goodness sakes!"

He balled up his fist and pounded on the door with the strength of a vibrant, indignant man. I heard him as he hollered and yelled and demanded to be let in. I saw him slow and stumble and sink to the marbled ground, breathless as he realized that the front door of the High Court that no longer welcomed Americans, no longer welcomed its icons either.

It was late Sunday in late spring, and there was no one on First Street Northeast to help the old man up. Not one living soul. So the Chief Justice limped down those forty-four steps and headed toward Union Station, old again. Infirm again. He lifted his arm in a half-hearted wave, his fingers twisted. I watched him as he shuffled toward the departing trains. And disappeared.

About the author:

Vanessa Orlando is a two-time recipient of the Maryland Writers Association Short Fiction Prize and a Georgia Associated Press Feature writing award. She was one of five writers selected for the Manitoba Writer's Guild's Emerging Writers Program in 2000. Her short story When Sara Looks Up was made into a short film by Columbia College Chicago in 2004. Her most recent work has been published in News Lines from the Old Line State (Maryland Writers Association) and Enhanced Gravity: More Fiction by Washington Area Women (Paycock Press, Arlington). Both are available on Amazon. She lives in Annapolis, Maryland with four dogs, two cats and one husband.

THE RAINBOW TREE

©2012 by Mary Smith

That Christmas of 1959, from the moment she spotted the aluminum tree, my mother thought that it was the most beautiful thing she had ever seen. All that glittery, shiny metal made it stand out like a guiding radiance, drawing her in to the store to buy.

It was on display in the Meredith Furniture Store window. The tree had been put up the first week of December as a uniqueness item for Christmas and wasn't selling too well. People were used to the live trees that could be found in any ranch pasture, or those lined up for sale downtown in front of the grocery store.

During the store hours, the tree glittered in the natural light of day and looked very ordinary and sort of bland, really. It looked like what it was: a bunch of metal rods with pieces of aluminum stuck on them.

But the evening my mother first saw the tree with only the store display fixtures glowing softly behind it, it became a work of art. The store had closed at five and all the lights, except a dim one for security, were turned off for the day, and that tree took on the luster of a precious stone. The tree came with an electrically powered wheel which was fixed with red, green, and blue panels and, when switched on, rotated in front of a special light bulb. As the wheel turned, the different colors would reflect on the metal of the tree, making it change colors accordingly with the turn of the wheel.

The wheel was a must since regular Christmas lights couldn't be strung on the tree. Back then, most tree lights were large screw-in types and there was really no place to attach them to the metal tree. Matter of fact, after buying the thing, mother discovered that not many decorations *could* be placed on it. There just wasn't anywhere for the hooks to go, and it seemed everything she tried just tore the metal 'leaves' off.

So, mothers beautiful tree, after that first year, was retired to the storage shed, where eventually the mice and squirrels that invaded there every year shredded the aluminum until all that was left was bare metal rods. I never knew what happened to the frame, but I suspect that Dad threw it away on a garbage day when mother wasn't around.

That has been many years ago, and those trees didn't last long at all. They became a passing fad that marked an era of being 'modern' or even 'space age.'

I was driving down a street lined with thrift stores the other day, when I happened to glance at one window, and there, in full view amidst the usual wares, was one of those trees.

I think of my mother all the time with fondness and love, but the moment I saw that tree I felt her stronger than I have ever before. I could hear her saying—as she said on that first night that she discovered the tree in the furniture store window—"Isn't that beautiful? Just look at the colors! It looks like a Christmas rainbow."

I resisted the urge to pull into the parking lot and go inside the shop to inquire the price of the tree. What I would have done with it, I'm not sure, but the longing was strong to have that tree. Maybe there's more of Mom in me than I thought. I didn't go back, however, and as I drove away, I glanced one last time through the rearview at the rainbow tree and said a mental goodbye to it, and my mother, and a long-ago Christmas when the new and modern just didn't work out so well.

About the author:

Chilly, rainy days always make me think of the years I was in school. Not the grown-up ones like high school, but the elementary time. That was an era when things were still simple for a seven-year-old girl who had never interacted with other children until she started first grade. My teachers name was Mrs. Eunice and she was the typical first grade teacher in looks and voice and attitude. Mrs. Eunice was the paragon of patience and tolerance as far as I'm concerned since she dealt with us all in a kind and motherly way-- all the while attempting to teach us what was needed to know for the future.

First grade was when most kids of that time actually learned to read since there was no such thing as kindergarten. My parents had never taken the time to teach me ahead of school, being not excessively educated themselves. That first little paperback reader that had Dick, Jane and Spot on the cover captivated me and I caught on fast how to read all those simple words. From that moment on, I was hooked and all through my school years I read everything I could get my hands on beginning in the school's limited library, and later the small county one located downtown in the courthouse.

I spent many hours browsing both places and all the while gaining the desire to write myself, especially the mysteries. This was a desire that I've never really been able to do anything with until now and the push is strong not so much to become well known, but to at least have been read and enjoyed by someone somewhere.

NUMBER ONE MUNCHING LANE
©2012 by J. E. Moore

The year was 1902. The location was the Marlbury Orphanage in the countryside outskirts of the bustling, ever-expanding birthplace of American independence: Philadelphia, Pennsylvania. The converted institution, originally constructed in 1841 as a hospital and sanitarium for disabled war veterans, had been adeptly administered by Mister Silas Huntington and his loyal staff for the past twelve years.

Times were good. Overall, America was prospering and the adoption rate had been going well for the children of six years and under. However, sometimes the older ones required a little different attention in order to dispose of them...

"Mary had a little lamb, little lamb," Katie sang softly to herself, "its fleece was white as snow." She was a happy child, as happy as one could be while growing up in a crowded county orphanage filled with a hundred other unwanted or unclaimed little souls. Katie was ten years old—four years beyond the prime-select age group—and she was resigned to never being placed with a foster family due to her frightening orange hair and dull brown eyes. 'New parents' always chose the youngest, prettiest, or blue-eyed children first. That was the way it was—akin to picking the cutest kittens out of a litter. Of course, the big, ugly wart on the end of her nose didn't help matters either, but then everyone had some problem, didn't they?

Katie dropped both her buckets onto the hard, packed dirt with a thud. She then stepped up on top of a fruit crate, reached down, picked up one of the containers, and threw its contents over her shoulder into the waiting five-foot high, two-wheeled, wooden trash wagon. While doing so, she wondered if she would see Mister MacIntosh today. Probably not, she had only a few minutes left before they rang the bell for class and he could arrive at any time on these Monday mornings; weather, road and horse permitting.

It certainly was a treat for her when she got to see him. He'd open the padlocked, large double gates in the rear of the compound, ride in, circle around and swap his empty wagon with the now filled, stinky one. He'd carefully replace the fruit crate right next to the new trash wagon; he knew a small person, usually a girl, was assigned to this particular chore. Katie had spoken to him quite a few times over the last couple of years and knew the fellow better than any other 'insider.' He was a nice, old Irish (whatever that was) man who had a heavy accent which she couldn't always understand. Sometimes if she was lucky, he would let her pet his horse, Cleo. It was fun. There were no animals allowed in the orphanage grounds, not even cats to kill the mice. The county welfare administrators were afraid some of the 'more aggressive' children would harm them.

Once, long ago, she dared to ask Mister MacIntosh if she could go outside the gates to see what was there, and maybe touch a tree or something green, but he said, "Sorry, no, m'darlin'. I can't do that." Being a kind man and father, he went on to explain he would like to but if that happened he could lose his job, and jobs were *very* hard for Irishmen to come by. She said, "I understand," but she didn't.

Katie threw the second bucket over. A few scraps caught the top edge of the buckboard and dropped back toward her, falling to the ground. "Oops." She jumped off her perch to retrieve them—no garbage was to be left scattered about. Mister Huntington required perfection for everything. His rules demanded all children complete their chores with thoroughness, or appropriate punishment would be applied. "This is not a high-class city slicker child care center," he lectured. "We will be neat and clean, or else!"

Katie scooped the fallen items quickly into the bucket. As she did her eye caught an unusual looking object lying on the ground between the crate and the wagon. It appeared to be a short, beige, worm-like thing. She was positive it wasn't anything she had brought. "What's this?" She picked it up, inspected, and rolled it in her palm. It wasn't alive, so she decided to dispose of it with her other trash. She was about to re-sling the bucket but then thought twice about it. Katie placed her unusual find aside and decided to have a grown-up examine it also. After all, it couldn't really be what it looked like. Could it?

While walking back to the main building and passing by one of the old brick classrooms, her concentration was broken by Jimmy, who was beating erasers against the wall. She said what was logical to her, "Hello, Jimmy. Are you being punished again?"

"Nah, what makes you say a thing like that?" he answered in defense. "This is a *good* chore, a reward. It shows that Headmaster Blackburn likes me," he falsely asserted.

"Yeah, sure," Katie dismissed, and returned to staring into her bucket.

He noticed her preoccupation. "Hey, whatcha got in there? Something neat? A frog?" he spoofed. "Lemme see." Jimmy rushed over, peeked in, then frowned. "Huh...?" Pulling out its contents and holding it up in the light, he stated, "It looks like a finger to me. Whatcha doing with a finger?"

"A finger? That's what *I* thought," answered Katie. "I'm taking it inside. Put it back in the bucket, please."

"Uh, okay, in a minute." Jimmy sniffed the suspected dead piece of meat and wrinkled his nose. "See this brown stain on the end? That's dried blood. Yuck!" He squinted, a puzzled look of recognition crossed his face. "Hey, wait a minute! This is Oggie's finger. Where'd you get it?"

"Huh?" she questioned. "Are you sure? I don't think Oggie lives here anymore."

"He did last week!" Jimmy countered. "And, he had all his fingers. Where'd you find this?"

"By Mister MacIntosh's trash wagon. Why do you think that finger's Oggie's?"

"See the freckles?" he directed. "Oggie had freckles everywhere...even on his rear end," he snorted as he dropped the severed appendage back into the bucket. "Where'd you say you were taking it? Are you gonna show it to a teacher?"

"Yes, I was thinking about Miss Applebee."

"Miss Applebee? Yeah. I guess she's a good choice...better than most," surmised Jimmy. "Okay, go find Miss Applebee, but don't tell her or nobody else that I talked to you. I'm supposed to be cleaning erasers. Agreed?" Katie nodded. "Tell you what, girl: I think that finger's got a story to tell. Meet me here at the same time tomorrow and we'll look for some more clues. I got lotsa free time tomorrow. Maybe we'll find an arm or leg...or Oggie's head filled with worms!"

Katie's eyes grew wide and her jaw dropped as she emitted a frightened, "Eeek!"

"Silly little girl, I'm just afunnin' ya."

Katie quickly scurried away to find Miss Applebee, who she was sure would calm her newly risen fears, which Jimmy had instilled in her. Yes, Miss Anabelle Applebee would know and explain everything. She treated the children with kindness, which was far different from the other workers here and the kids believed whatever she said. Even better, the young woman was attractive, smart, and smiled a lot. In fact, she was the only adult here who *ever* smiled. Maybe that's why all the children liked to be around her.

Katie soon found her working in the school's library and offered her bucket without comment.

"Oh, my. What do we have here, Katie?"

"Is it Oggie's?" she blurted.

After studying the finger, the young girl's custodian knelt to Katie's level and said slowly, as if searching for the correct words,

"Yes, dear, its Oggie's...or rather it was. He's gone now."

Katie's arched eyebrows asked, "Why?"

"He was adopted four days ago, late at night."

"Adopted?" Katie repeated. "Oggie's been taken? But he was so ugly..." Miss Applebee frowned. "Sorry, ma'am. I mean, we all thought he was too old and looked...er...not so pretty."

"Ah, well, I understand what you mean, Katie. Perhaps 'adopted' is the wrong word. Let's just say some long-distant relative...an uncle...came for him."

For some unknown reason Katie felt as if Miss Applebee was making up her story as she went along. To appease her? To fool her? If so, why? She peeked at the finger again.

"Oh, that!" exclaimed Miss Applebee. "The finger and the blood, of course...an accident happened...while Oggie was boarding the carriage. Yes, an accident!" seemingly pleased with herself. "The horses bolted. They were frightened by a flash of lightning. The carriage jerked, he fell, and was caught in the ironwork. His finger was ripped off in an instant, just like that!"— clapping her hands once. "Very unfortunate. His...uncle...pinched it and tied off the stub. They drove him into town to have the doctor stitch it up." She paused for effect, "Oggie was very brave, but still happy to leave...in spite of the tragedy. We all will miss him very much. I'm sorry you had to find out about it this way. Apparently, the finger wasn't disposed of properly." Giving her best, condescending smile, "Is there anything else, Katie?"

"No, ma'am. Thank you, Miss Applebee."

"Leave the bucket here. I'll take care of it. You run off now to your class. It must be starting soon."

Katie sat in her classroom with three other girls about her own age. No teacher was present, there seldom was. An old, decrepit science book had been placed on each desk top. Each student had to read it for two hours, no talking permitted. An attendant would come in and announce when the class was finished. There would then be an hour for chores before the next class. Without the least bit of interest she flipped through the thirty-year old pages and wondered why she hadn't heard the storm or Oggie's screaming three nights ago. "But then," she reasoned, "Miss Applebee said it was late at night and I must have been asleep."

After the class Katie was on her way to the cafeteria for her next chore and happened to pass by a window overlooking the front courtyard entranceway. Mister Weolf, the grounds keeper, stood aside the roadway, a shovel laid at his feet, head bowed low, and his hands clutching his cap in a wad to his chest. He appeared timid...and afraid. Directly in front of him was Miss Applebee, wailing and flailing her arms all about. Katie couldn't hear the words she was screaming, but Mister Weolf, a giant of a man, looked so assailed and distressed, Katie thought he was going to break down in tears. The empty trash bucket lay at their feet. Miss Applebee waved Oggie's finger in his face, then threw it down and ground it into the dirt with the heel of her shoe. She next pointed at the shovel, said a few more choice words, and then stormed off.

Katie wanted to see more but had to rush to the cafeteria before the cook became mad and threw the overflowing garbage against the kitchen walls. She would have to clean it up and not get dinner.

The following day:

"And that's what happened," Katie related to Jimmy.

"Wow, I can't believe little Miss Applebee would talk to Mister Weolf like that! He's so big and scary. I've never ever seen him smile...or even heard him speak," marveled Jimmy while shaking his head.

"I told you true, Jimmy."

"Yeah, okay."

"And what I told you about Oggie's finger, too," she added.

"Well...if Miss Applebee says so, it must be true," he conceded. "Maybe."

"Jimmy..."

"Hey, c'mon. She's one of the *girls* teachers. I don't know her that good." Playing devil's advocate, "Tell me this, Katie. Don't you think it's kinda' strange so many *ugly* kids get adopted late at night? I swear it's been going on ever since I've been here and probably before then, too. They disappear, and we never hear from them again. Whatcha think of that, little girl?"

Not agreeing with his assessment, "We never hear from *anyone* who leaves here, Jimmy. That's not so strange. No one wants to come back to see this place again."

"Umm, well, er," Jimmy murmured.

"And," Katie added, "did you ever consider maybe Mister Huntington doesn't want us to see anyone leave? I know I would be very sad to see them go. I truly would."

"Yeah, maybe so," he passively agreed, for the moment. But, being a suspicious-type boy, he added, "And maybe not so." He scanned the surrounding area. "Guess there's no reason to snoop around the trash wagon now. I'm sure Mister Weolf picked up any other loose tidbits or evidence after he got fussed out."

As they wandered back toward the main building and far away from the wagon, Jimmy stopped. "Hey, look at that!"

"What?" Katie asked.

Jimmy pointed and noted, "The cellar storeroom door is unlocked." The padlock hung open. "Never seen that before...and the door's open a crack. Let's look inside."

"I dunno," fretted Katie. "I don't think we're supposed to be here. We could get into trouble. What if a grown-up comes? We might get a beating." She lamented, "Worse than that, what if Mister Weolf comes! He'd get blamed for leaving it open, and who knows what he'd do to us after getting fussed out by Miss Applebee."

"Don't worry, it won't happen. I saw the big, bad Mister Weolf leave to go to town an hour ago and all the other teachers are doing somethin' else. Stop acting like a fraidy-cat girl."

Jimmy slowly pulled back the door. It was dark inside, but the outside light showed stairs leading downward. They both put their heads into the doorway.

"I don't like it," whispered Katie. "It's spooky."

"Nah, it ain't so bad. I can see the floor. There must be a torch or somethin' burning down there." He gently grabbed her arm, "C'mon, let's go in."

In no hurry, and one behind the other, they descended. There were no handrails, which prompted from Katie, "Boy, if you didn't know these stairs were here, you could fall and break your neck."

"Maybe that's what *really* happened to Oggie," touted Jimmy. "Maybe he and all the other missing children are hidden down here...their bones stashed in a storeroom filled with giant, hairy spiders! Eeee...ohhh," he teased.

They arrived at the bottom, the floor was worn-smooth stone, the air felt dank and still. There were two tunnels. One was faintly lit with a few scattered candles, the other appeared pitch-black. Each tunnel entrance had an iron-bar door which was opened fully against the wall. An unlit oil lamp hung between them on a peg.

"Too bad I don't have any matches on me now, we could use the lamp," commented Jimmy.

"We're not allowed to have matches. You know that."

"Oh, yeah," he giggled. "I forgot. But it don't matter none; we got enough light to see down that one tunnel," gesturing to his right. He set off, his boyish curiosity leading the way with Katie in close pursuit. After a few dozen yards Jimmy said, "I don't see any storage area. It must lead to a coal bin." His voice raised an octave in excitement, "Yeah! A coal bin means there's a dump chute and its top opening would have to be on the other side of the wall. We can climb up the chute and escape to the city!" He picked up his pace only to soon run into the path's dead-end. "Shucks," disappointed. "It's not here." He spat on the ground. "There's no way out."

"Sorry, Jimmy. But look, there's a secret room over here." Katie pointed and waved her hand in the open, dark doorway. "See?"

Jimmy retrieved a near burned-out candle from a tunnel ledge and thrust it inside to reveal a sparsely furnished room containing a table with four chairs surrounding it. They stepped inside. "Whew! What's that stinky smell?" asked Jimmy.

"It smells like rotten old meat," answered Katie. "Very *bad* old meat. I've smelled things like this when I work in the kitchen. Thank goodness they never cook it; they throw it out. Maybe, this is where they dump it."

"Down here? I don't think so," retorted Jimmy. "Phew," as he pinched his nose. He held the light toward a wooden box sitting in the corner next to a large, ancient cast-iron cooking pot turned upside down. "I think the smell is coming from over this way." He waved the candle inside the box. It was empty except for some brownish gunk on the bottom, which stank very badly. Jimmy's foot kicked a heavy gunny sack marked LYE.

Katie read the labeling. "This must have been a salted-meat locker once upon a time and they were trying to clean it. This whole place looks very old. Maybe it's from the Civil War."

"Shoot, it could be from the *Revolutionary* War," countered Jimmy. "We're outside Philadelphia, remember? As for their cleaning the place, they didn't do a very good job. If I did a chore this bad I'd get a whippin' with a switch for sure." The candle flickered out. "Oh, no! Let's get outta here." Katie agreed wholeheartedly. With quick, probing hands they felt their way out of the room and back into the dimming tunnel. "We'd better hurry, all the candles are going out!" They scampered back to the stairs. Before going back up, Jimmy gave a quick glance at the other tunnel to the left.

Katie, reading his mind, asked, "Do you think *that* one goes under the wall to a coal chute?"

"Nah, it's going in the wrong direction...*away* from the wall," her friend answered.

A few moments later, at the cellar entrance, "Well, I guess that didn't lead to anything, did it, Jimmy? Nothing, except we could have gotten caught and been in big trouble. I've decided from now on I'm not going to explore anymore secret places. It's too dangerous."

"Yeah, well okay," Jimmy agreed while admonishing her at the same time. "Don't tell anyone what we done and especially that I was with you. I'm already on probation. I could git a belt whippin' and tossed in the Hole for a month." He patted her shoulder, "Thanks for going with me, Katie. See ya around."

As time passed, Katie became more dissatisfied with Miss Applebee's previous explanation—it sounded too 'made up'. She began asking the other children about the storm—no one seemed to have heard—and the mysterious carriage which came for Oggie. Katie wouldn't let the sleeping dog lie. Even though she tried to be careful not to ask questions when the adults were around, they still got wind of it and began to look at her with a suspicious eye.

About a week later, she was working inside the Main Office's front foyer when a well-dressed man and woman made an arrival. Katie piddled about with her cleaning in order to remain nearby, within earshot.

Mister Huntington met them at the reception desk with, "Good day, Silas Huntington at your service. May I assist you?"

The pair were trying to locate a boy, John Long, a distant nephew of theirs, for his grandparents in New York. They were just seeking information to aid a family's random search of the eastern big cities. No one actually had any idea where the boy truly was and prior investigations had drawn a blank.

Mister Huntington acted compassionately; he parried their questions and assured them the lad was not, nor had ever been, at his facility. After politely conversing with them for a few minutes, he bade, "A good day and good luck in your venture."

Katie, upon hearing his send-off, piped up and said, "I knew him."

The couple appeared surprised. Mister Huntington's reaction was more diverse: his mustache and ears immediately began twitching. He was clearly far beyond mere surprise, he was aghast. "I'm sure the girl is in error," he stammered. "I know every child who has ever been under my supervision." Giving Katie a sharp look, "Run along young lady and stop bothering these nice people."

"One moment please," interjected the man. "You say you knew

this boy?"

"Yes, sir...yes, ma'am," she answered.

"Why? How?" they chimed.

"Because of his name. John said his name was 'Long', but he was 'short' for his age. I thought it was odd and funny."

"Yes, indeed," agreed the man. "I see that it would certainly strike you as such."

"What else, m'dear?" plied his wife.

"I don't remember anything else. We didn't speak much after he arrived because the boys and girls are kept separate...except in a few classes and the cafeteria."

"And when did you last see the lad...?" began the gentleman.

"Enough! Untrue! Entirely wrong," interrupted Mister Huntington in a huff. "*As* I stated before, the boy has never been here and I can *prove* it." He retrieved his Registration Ledger and hurriedly flipped through its pages. With a stiff upper lip he displayed the entries. "As you can see for yourself, there has never been a child admitted by that name. However, there *was* a boy with a similar name a few years ago: a John Louder. Perhaps he is the one Katie is *confused* with." He shrugged his shoulders, then glared at the girl. Gritting his teeth, "As I *said*, run along, *dear*. Mister Huntington was clearly infuriated being contradicted by anyone, especially a simple child. "We will talk again later, Katie, and I will *refresh* your memory as to how we do things here." With a strained smile to the couple, "As you can see, children's accounts are neither factual nor reliable. I apologize for her misleading you." The couple left without further comment.

Katie sprinted away, putting as much distance between herself and Mister Huntington as she could. She knew she would receive a bruising, blood-to-the-skin paddling that night, but now she had even more questions to ask.

Days passed, and as they did the living conditions worsened for Katie greatly. She was given more and difficult punishment chores, those normally assigned to the boys, increased separation from the other children, and isolation at night. And, of course, she received corrective, physical discipline on a regular basis to re-educate her in "Children should be seen and not heard." She cried a lot, but her spirit had not been broken. She never faltered and mentioned Jimmy's name to lessen her load.

Then, it stopped. Miss Applebee became officiously civil again, although she wasn't friendly, as before. Even mean old Mister Huntington and the other staff members ceased scolding her. In fact, other than Miss Applebee, none of the staff would speak to her at all, or even look her in the eye. She was being shunned by everyone except Mister Weolf, who became just the opposite. He had never spoken to her before, but now went out of his way to make such pleasant comments as "You're looking nice today, Miss Katie," or "Maybe this will be your *special* day, Miss Katie," meaning the day to be adopted. He'd give her arm a gentle squeeze or a playful poke in the tummy. His face and eyes smiled, but his mouth did not fully reflect his happiness, his lips remained closed tight.

She concluded the standoffish Mister Weolf had observed her unwarranted mistreatment and tried to make her feel better in his own oafish way. *Could he be a new friend who's embarrassed by his bad teeth, or is it he has none at all?* Katie wondered.

A few days later, after all the children had gone to bed at the usual hour of eight p.m., Miss Applebee came to her bedside and awakened her. "Shush, Katie. Arise and get dressed."

Being quiet and careful not to disturb the other sleeping girls, Katie quickly did as she was ordered. Her mind was aflutter. This had never happened before. Was she in trouble again or was Mister Weolf right? Had someone come to claim her? Were people going to take her away to a new home? She became so excited, but held her tongue and expressions in. She could hardly wait until they got into the hallway so she could ask.

Finally, "Miss Applebee, Miss Applebee," she sputtered, "Is it *my* turn?"

"What? Your turn for what?" the woman repeated.

"Yes, my turn to go. It's nighttime, so the other kids won't see me leave."

"Oh, *that* nighttime. No, it's not your turn." Katie was very disappointed. "Something unexpected has come up and we require your assistance in a special chore immediately. It must be completed before the morning, so hush-up now." Then, for no apparent reason her demeanor suddenly became quite stern, "And don't give me any of your sass, girl," she snapped. "Do as I say!"

Surprised and taken aback by Miss Applebee's abrupt mood swing, Katie bemoaned to herself, *More work. I'm back to being punished again.* Inwardly, she was crushed she wasn't leaving the orphanage, and fell in a silent stride, head downcast, behind the woman as directed.

They came to the cellar door, the same one she and Jimmy had ventured into weeks ago. "The cellar?"

"You know this place?" challenged the adult.

"Uh," Katie stammered. "Some kids said it was here."

"What else did they say?"

"Oh...er...nothing. I don't know anything else about it," Katie lied to protect herself and Jimmy.

"You children shouldn't be poking around in restricted areas. You could get hurt. Do you understand?"

"Yes, ma'am."

Soon they were at the bottom of the stairs, where Miss Applebee struck a match and lit the lantern which was still hanging between the passageways. Katie could see a faint light at the far end of the left tunnel, this time the right one was dark.

"What do you want me to do, Miss Applebee?" The woman stared back as if she hadn't understood the question. "You said you had a special chore for me."

"Oh, yes. I did, didn't I?" She raised the lantern toward the left passageway. "We have to move some...old furniture up to the courtyard for trash pick-up tomorrow morning."

"Is it big...or heavy?" Katie asked. "I'm just a little girl. Is Mister Weolf going to help us?"

"Mister Weolf? Oh, I'm sure we'll see him shortly and he'll be a big help," informed her mentor. "And believe me, we know exactly *what* you are," with a twinkle in her eye. "Step this way, please." And as Katie did the woman closed and locked the iron-barred gate behind them. *Clank!* "We don't want any anyone to stray down here and get lost."

Traveling down this corridor seemed more eerie than the other one, because there were no scattered candles to lead the way as before. Katie cocked her head, thinking she heard indistinguishable voices coming from the far end. Peeking around Miss Applebee, she saw light coming from another side room. *This tunnel must be built just like the other one*, she thought.

Miss Applebee paused at the doorway, then turned around and roughly seized Katie's arm. "We're here, dearie," and shoved the child inside.

The room was identical to the first, containing a table with four chairs and a wooden box on the floor next to a giant cooking pot, this one upright and with a blazing fire beneath it. Candles in the corners of the room and on the table revealed Misters Huntington, Blackburn, and Weolf sitting there; the fourth chair was vacant.

"Hello, Annabelle," said Mister Blackburn. "Did you bring us a treat tonight?"

"A good evening to you, gentlemen, and did I ever! Just look who I brought for dinner...our own little Miss Busybody." She nudged Katie closer to the center of the room. The candlelight danced on the men's glistening faces. Miss Applebee gave an uncharacteristic, throaty laugh, "Just call me your gourmet pimp, boys!"

The three men howled in glee and stamped their feet in delighted anticipation. The woman then slammed the door closed behind them. Mister Weolf flashed a big smile, revealing pearly white filed-to-a-point teeth. Katie's eyes darted to the other two men's open, grinning mouths. Their teeth were the same!

Frightened, she jumped back, bumping into Miss Applebee's legs. Her mouth dropped as she squealed, "Nooo!"

"Ha! The boys *are* scary, aren't they?" quipped Miss Applebee. "Sometimes they can act like such animals. Not everyone uses a knife and fork as I do, sweetie"

Mister Huntington said, "I'm very glad to have you here for dinner, Katie. I've been waiting some time for this."

Which prompted her new friend, Mister Weolf, to rise from his seat with a meat cleaver in his hand. He gushed, "I hope she's more tender than Oggie was."

Bon appetite.

About the author:

J.E. Moore lives with his wife of twenty-four years, Joyce, in Davie, south Florida with their numerous grandchildren in close proximity. After retiring as a telephone company electronic technician and also being a former police officer, he is now able to fully apply his long-gained experience and expertise to his writings. John credits his success so far to the encouragement and support of his loving soul-mate and family.

With a collection of sci-fi/paranormal/horror short stories and an accompanying full-length SF novel, both 'ready for launch', he is presently seeking a literary agent—but then, aren't we all!

FOR CHRIS, I'M SORRY THIS IS LATE
©2012 by Kathleen Ratcliffe

Regrets. I've had many. I couldn't even list them all on a few pages. We all have shoulda-coulda-wouldas, yet we carry on. Even if we got a do over, it would produce the same result. Do we ever learn from our laments or just keep repeating?

I walked into my circuit boxing class pleased with myself for attending this week. As it's only held on Wednesdays I hardly ever miss this class. But it was too hot last week, I was too lazy, my husband was home, there were a slew of great reasons. Besides, it's not like I don't exercise almost daily. So I pushed myself out the door this week, wearing my guilt like a truant schoolgirl does. In my haste to leave, I forgot my boxing gloves. I hoped Chris would bring his extra set. He almost always does.

Barely through the door the instructor looked up at me and said, "You weren't here last week." I was preparing myself for an onslaught of his abuse. Kevin likes torturing his students, especially his regulars: Chris, John and myself. So, while preparing my clever comeback, I was not ready for what came next.

Kevin is a jokester, a bit of a smart alec, in a harmless way. In the year that I've known him, he's been serious exactly never. I learned early that he can feign being stern for only seconds at a time.

"Something really bad happened," Kevin said. The look on his face told me he wasn't kidding this time. "Chris passed away.

Looks like it was a massive heart attack." Kevin went on to say that no one was sure how long Chris had been dead when they found him. They *found* him! He was found dead at home. A whole scenario played out in my head.

Kevin continued telling the story while I tried to digest the crux. Chris passed away. Was he even forty? Chris died. Chris is dead. We will never see him in this class or anywhere else. Regulars and drop-ins always agreed that there wasn't a greater guy than Chris.

It's not like he was my best friend, or even *a* friend. He was an acquaintance. I wasn't hot for him. I hadn't even thought of becoming good friends with the guy. But at that moment, for some reason, I found myself wishing that I had gotten to know him a little better. People die daily. That's a fact. I've been an emergency room nurse for over twenty years so wouldn't you think I'd be used to it...jaded even?

Class went on, we went through the routines like usual. I kept thinking about this person. He died alone. Kevin told us that the funeral was extremely sad and very crowded. Grieving family and friends said Chris will be sorely missed.

At the end of the grueling workout, and it is a tough class, I had a few more questions about Chris. Kevin had known him for a few years. Not well, just in class. Chris had been coming to circuit boxing for the last five years. John, another regular, knew him only as a classmate. They started this course around the same time. While they seemed to be friends, it was only here in the gym. They spoke of getting together to go fishing, but it never happened.

Usually I feel on top of the world at the end of these sessions. I am pleased with myself for being able to complete such strenuous exercise. Tonight I was fixated on this news.

As I said before, I am no stranger to the end of life. The very first night I worked in emergency, two young boys died when the car their mother was driving was broadsided by who else but a drunk driver. The mom was taken right to surgery. I still recall thinking, *Oh help her, please. She doesn't even know that her children are gone.* Believe me, that sickening feeling stayed with me for a few days, until the next fatality.

Since that time I've witnessed many other deaths. After a while they start to blend together. Many are sudden and tragic, leaving family and friends shattered by the loss. Even the ones people expect, whether as a result of old age or serious illness are devastating in their way. Each takes its toll on the survivors. Famous people die and we are saddened even though we know them only peripherally.

Since people's passing surrounds me, I am rarely moved by any of it, sudden or otherwise. Fatalities have been a part of my job almost daily. Not to sound morbid, but death *is* what life is all about.

So here I sit, in a bar of all places. Funny, the last time I went to a bar was...I don't know, maybe ten years ago. Maybe. Here's the best—I'm not even drinking, at least not alcohol. For some reason I wanted to get bombed. Now that is no big feat, since it only takes two light beers to put me to sleep. Why I thought I could sit and drink for hours escapes me. Once in here, I realized that a drunken stupor, even a partial one, is not what I seek. So I'm drinking water. Tap water, at that. I thoughtfully put a twenty-dollar bill on the bar so I wouldn't get booted for loitering.

It's smoky in here, my eyes are watering, my clothes already reek of tobacco. I don't know a soul in here and am being eyed with mild curiosity by those whom I assume are the established patrons. No one's really paying me any serious attention. It's apparent I mean no harm.

For some reason this is the perfect place for me tonight. My husband is away on business. While it doesn't usually bother me to have the house to myself, I just didn't want to be alone. The safety of home was not appealing, most unusual for me. I craved a room full of strangers. There was something soothing about anonymity. Years ago I might have suggested that Kevin, John, and myself go to have "one for Chris." But we've never socialized together, none of us knew Chris that well, and it just didn't feel right. They probably would have excuses anyhow.

Bartender is checking on me, as is his duty. He's satisfied that I am fine. What he is thinking—or if he is—I don't know or care. Thankfully he lets me be. A white noise results from customers' chatter, three TVs, and continuous beverage pouring. Glasses hit the thick wooden bar with a dull thud, a wordless request for a refill. A haze-covered mirror stares back at me, revealing distortions of those seated here. The stools, though worn, are still padded enough and comfortable. I'm not the first to be content to settle in.

My mind, which has been blank for the past hour is now ready to contemplate that which brings me here.

Chris, why does your death bother me so much? I knew nothing about you. No, I actually *did* know a few things. We engaged in insignificant conversation. I only saw you at the weekly classes and never intended more than that. But you were my first "friend" in there and encouraged me, especially after that initial tough workout.

We rushed in to class, rushed out at the end. And that too is life. That's what I do. That's what everybody does. We keep the force field up. We friend, we like, we tweet, but the subject of interest is "me." So, is that what I'm doing now? Am I making this poor guy's death about me?

Oh, *I* feel so sad. *I* feel so horrible. How will *I* ever get through this? So, have I made this sad news about myself?

After I don't know how long, I answer: "No!" No, not this time. It is clear, even in here in the tavern fog, this is not about me. It is a statement of life in our busy little worlds. We have a quota of people we allow inside and no one over and above that may enter.

You know, I even think my husband would have enjoyed Chris's company. As I said earlier, we all liked the guy. It's one thing to say it. The chance was there and then gone. There was no warning, no game show theme, no last minute of play, as time expired.

I mourn now for a missed opportunity. I mourn because I have allowed death to become so expected that I forget to live. Going through daily activities is just that. We are nothing but living, breathing robots, never deviating from our routine. I guard my precious time doling out meager portions only to those I love. No one else gets a pass.

I'd love to say that this will change my life. I'd love to say that I will reach out to others and really take interest in them. I'm sad now because that will not be. My templated life will continue as before.

It's five of two, closing time. I lift my drink to Chris, wherever he is, and swig my water. Without drama, I place my empty glass on the bar. No one looks; they are concerned with their own business. I slip out unnoticed.

About the author:

Kathleen Ratcliffe is a registered nurse whose career is divided between working clinically in a cardiac catherization laboratory and providing education to medical professionals all over the United States. Employed by a small company in Pennsylvania, her job involves composing educational material and instruction of the clinical aspects of invasive cardiology.

During the past fifteen years she became a single parent, studied to become a registered nurse and raised two children with the help of her wonderful mother. She then pursued a bachelor's degree while working to support her family. After years of writing papers and presentations related to nursing, she has been afforded the time to go back to writing fiction. Several stories are complete and others are in progress.

As sports editor for her high school paper, she attended a journalism seminar for high school editors at the Catholic University in Washington D.C. It was there where her fervor for writing expanded.

Kathleen will be resuming her studies for a post-grad degree in nursing in the spring. She hopes to be teaching in the near future, and looks forward to continuing writing, as well.

The proud mother of two children, her son is a PhD candidate in anthropology at Temple University. Her daughter is a student at Montgomery County Community College.

Besides writing, Kathleen's interests include running, cycling and yoga. Her husband, who is also a registered nurse, introduced her to the world of triathlon several years ago. Helping her conquer her fear of open water swimming, he made her realize that anything is possible if you try.

Kathleen was married on 10/10/10.

MARBLES
©2012 by Joseph L. Rose

"Hey Cindy, isn't that your little brother sitting down over there on the curb? It sounds like he's crying."

"Oh my God," I said, and ran to the street as fast as I could. "What's wrong, Joey?" I asked.

"I've lost my marbles," he said.

"Oh, that. Heck, Joey, I've known that for years."

"That's not funny," said little Eddie who had been sitting there next to Joey. Then he added, "He lost them to Butch, the big kid."

I looked over at Joey and said, "How many did you lose?"

"All of them; and Mom is going to be mad, real mad, because she bought them for me yesterday. I was supposed to save them for the marble tournament next week."

"You don't need marbles for that," I said. "If you read the bulletin board like you're supposed to you would know that the school is going to provide all the marbles."

"Really," Eddie chimed in. "Well, that is all except the shooters. You have to provide your own and the rules also say that you can only use two."

"Mom's still going to be pissed at me," Joey said.

"How much do the marbles cost, Joey?" I asked.

"They're a dollar and seventy-five cents for a bag of a hundred, which also includes two shooters," Joey responded.

"What if I loan you the money to buy more, that way you can practice for the tournament?" I asked.

"Thank you, Cindy", he said, "but still don't tell Mom. She had already bought me three bags in the last two weeks.

"Where are they? What happened?" I said.

"Butch is what happened; he cheats!" Joey responded.

I walked Joey and Eddie to the little store on the corner to buy more marbles. Apparently Butch, a big sixth grade bully, had been playing with the fourth graders and winning their marbles away from them. I've watched my brother play several times and he is really pretty good. I challenged him one time; towards the end of summer before school started. We drew a large circle on the ground and dropped thirty marbles inside the circle. I then drew a straight line on the dirt next to the circle. We lagged for who would go first. Joey won. Joey used a steel shooter and knocked ten marbles out of the circle on his first shot. Then he took a regular shooter (twice the size of a marble) and quickly emptied the circle. I didn't even get a chance to shoot.

As we left the little store, I made Joey promise me not to play against Butch unless it was during the tournament; then he would stand a chance.

On Monday, Mrs. Hopkins went on the PA system to tell us about the upcoming marble tournament. It was going to be held Friday at one o'clock, with school being let out early for the special event. She said, "The marbles are being provided by the school. Well, sort of. Mrs. Clark, Mrs. Wilson, and I have been collecting marbles taken away from...bad boys...and the collection has grown to over three thousand! Tomorrow, you will each receive a list of tournament rules and, if you don't want to participate but know someone who does, a proxy—or vote—where you can select someone else. The top twenty vote getters will participate in the tournament. Good luck!"

The next day, Joey came running up to me with two proxies in his hands. "You going to vote for me?" he asked.

"What if I want to play, too?" I asked.

"Aw, come on, Sis," he said.

"Sure I will," I answered, then added, "A lot of boys and girls already know that you play really well, I'm sure that they will vote for you."

"I hope so," he said, and then handed me the rules for the tournament.

There were only four rules:

Rule #1– Each player will receive 100 marbles. Shooters are not supplied and will be limited to two shooters per player.

Rule #2 – Players will draw names to determine who they will play against. Names will be retained for the next draw.

Rule #3 – Lagging will determine which paired player will shoot first. Each player will start with 50 marbles in the circle. The winner will be the one with the majority of won marbles (for example: beginning with 100 marbles, the player with 51 or more marbles is the winner). Winners will keep all marbles knocked from the circle. Losing opponents will retain those marbles not yet lost.

Rule #4 – After first round of play, the remaining ten winners will draw names to determine their opponents. Play will continue until all participants have played. At that point, players with at least 50 marbles in their possession may challenge other players. The overall winner will be determined by the most marbles won during the tournament. All marbles won may be kept by the winning player.

THE WINNER WILL ALSO RECEIVE A LARGE TROPHY AND A $50 SAVINGS BOND.

TWO RUNNERS UP WILL EACH RECEIVE A SMALLER TROPHY.

It was one long week, but Friday finally came. The names of the participants were on the front office bulletin board, with kids standing six deep, everyone trying to see his or her name. Mrs. Wilson walked up and settled everyone down. Then she took the list off the bulletin board and starting reading the names. She began with the sixth grade.

After several names, she said, "Butch Hendricks," and I couldn't help myself but to say the "s" word. Then she read the fifth graders, and finally came to the fourth grade. "Joey Rodriguez" she called out and I saw Joey jump for joy, with several of his friends patting him on the back and congratulating him. Eddie had loaned him two of his shooters since Butch had won Joey's. They were admiring them as I walked up. I saw that one was a big gray steel ball, about an inch wide. The other was a white glass marble with yellow and gold stripes, about three quarters of an inch wide.

I wedged in between his admirers and congratulated him. I told him I would meet him at the school playground, next to the backstop. I knew they were going to use the baseball diamond for the tournament since it was covered with soft dirt.

At one o'clock sharp everyone gathered around the baseball diamond. There were four areas marked off about six feet apart. Inside the areas were four large circles, about two and a half feet apart. Mrs. Hopkins placed all the names in a hat, gave it a little shake, and then handed the hat over to Mrs. Wilson. All the names were drawn and Joey looked a little sad when he learned that he drew Bobby, a fifth grader. They then lined up so that Mrs. Hopkins could give them their bags of marbles. Mrs. Wilson went around and chose Joey to be the first player. He handed Mrs. Wilson his piece of paper, and she read off Bobby's name. They went to the circle close to the backstop. Bobby won the lag; he would shoot first.

Bobby counted out fifty marbles and placed them in the circle. Joey did the same, grouping them tight in the circle. Bobby got down on his knees and rested his hand right up close to the outside line of the circle, making sure his knuckles didn't go over the line. If they did, it would be considered a foul and it would then be Joey's turn.

Bobby's shot went towards the center of the circle and struck the marble that was close to him. No marbles went out of the circle. It was Joey's turn now and he got down on his knees, took that big steely of Eddie's and loped the marble high in the air, dropping down in the center of the circle, right on top of the group of marbles. They scattered in all directions. Eleven marbles left the circle and Joey gathered them up. Now, once inside the circle you must keep on playing until you either miss or don't knock a marble out of the circle. Using all his strength, Joey's next shot went straight at the cluster and knocked out eight more marbles.

I kept score; that made 19.

He swapped shooters now; breaking out the big glass marble. He aimed at three marbles, striking them hard, but only one left the circle. He now had twenty, and it was still his turn. He aimed at a cluster of about ten and fired again. Five went out of the circle.

Score: 25.

He stood up, went to the other side of the circle, got down on his knees, and just stayed there. Then he stood up, reached into his jeans pocket, and switched the glass shooter for the steely.

Then I saw what he was planning.

There were a group of about forty marbles yet untouched. He aimed right at them and with all his might shot that steely right into the cluster. They split apart, with fifteen leaving the circle on the other side.

Smart move, I thought. Score: 40.

He never gave Bobby a chance to shoot again. He had scored fifty-two when Mrs. Wilson told the boys to stop. He and Bobby shook hands.

Joey sat down on the bench next to me. I got us two sodas from the table next to the backstop. When I sat down again, Joey said, "I just drew Tommy."

"Okay," I said, "so what?"

"He's a *sixth* grader," Joey said.

"Oh," was my only response. I watched as Tommy and Joey lagged for who was going to go first. Joey won the lag and I could see he had a great big smile on his face. I think I knew what that little rascal had on his mind. Since Tommy had the advantage of height and strength, the only way to beat him was to not give him a chance to shoot. And Joey did just that; he racked up 56 marbles and then I saw Tommy walking straight for Joey. Tommy and I arrived at the same time.

"Nice game, huh, Tommy?" I said as I looked down at him. Tommy and I both played on the school's flag football team, and Tommy knew that if he wanted to get rough with little Joey he would have to go through his big sister first.

The games continued until there were only two players left: Butch and Joey. I don't know why, but I just had a feeling it was going to come out like this. The kids gathered all around, but kept real quiet. I heard Mrs. Hopkins tell Mrs. Wilson that this is the first time she had ever seen these kids this quiet. "We should have more marble tournaments," was her response.

One of the janitors came over and asked us all to stand back while he smoothed out a large area in the center of the diamond. He used a trashcan lid to make the circle and put eight wooden stakes around, and about six feet away from, the circle. Mrs. Wilson and Mrs. Hopkins tied red ribbons between the stakes. "Everyone please stay behind the ribbon," announced Mrs. Hopkins.

Joey lost the lag and didn't say a word, just moved over next to me on the far side. "What do you think, Sis?" he asked.

"Let him make his own mistakes," I said with a big smile. I saw Mrs. Hopkins nodding her head in agreement.

Butch used a big grey marble to break into the large cluster of marbles. Even though the cluster moved and a few marbles broke free from the pack, none left the circle.

It was Joey's turn and he took out his steely. I thought he was going to go for the middle of the pack, then I saw him shuffle his feet and lean towards his left. He aimed at a few marbles that had broken from the pack; no more than five or six, I thought. His shot glanced off the first marble and headed straight for the pack. The first marble he struck had enough momentum to knock four marbles out of the circle.

Score: Joey 4, Butch 0.

His steely had broken up the pack so there were small clusters of twenty to thirty marbles inside the circle. He shot that steely right smack into one of the smaller clusters and knocked out fifteen marbles.

Score: Joey 19, Butch 0.

The score was 32 to 15 when Joey failed to knock out any marbles from the circle. I looked down at the circle. Two marbles were right there on the line, the call could have gone either way. Butch aimed his shooter towards the pack again, but even though it hit hard, he failed to knock any out.

Joey got out his steely again and aimed it right at Butch's shooter. Joey's shooter struck hard and you could hear the crowd cheer when Butch's shooter broke in half and continued through the pack knocking out six more marbles.

Score: 38 to 15.

Mrs. Wilson came over and said that Butch could either replace his shooter or forfeit the game. Butch broke out another shooter and exchanged it with the broken one. Joey took aim again, this time impacting the pack hard enough for several marbles to head towards the edge of the circle. Butch had been sitting there alongside the circle with his hand just outside the chalk line. I saw him push the dirt towards the circle, just enough to make the edge of the line rise. He quickly removed his hand as the marbles approached the line.

This is what Joey had been trying to explain to me about Butch and his habit of cheating. As the marbles approached the outer circle, they slowed and stopped just before the line and rolled back inside the circle. Joey glanced over to my direction but didn't say a word.

It was now Butch's turn and he was able to knock out six more before his turn ended.

Score: Joey 38, Butch 21.

Joey moved once again to the opposite side of the circle, and Butch followed suit, making sure he was staying close to the circle.

I stopped watching Joey and kept my full attention now on Butch. Butch didn't waste a minute, placing his hand on the ground just outside the line. I watched as he again pushed dirt up against the outside of the circle. I looked towards the circle and saw two marbles leaving the center, heading toward the chalk line, but again stopping just before exiting the circle.

I was heading for Mrs. Wilson when Joey coughed loudly. I looked at him, and he was shaking his head. *Okay*, I thought, *it's your game!*

What took place next put Joey right up there with my list of heroes! After Butch failed to get any marbles out of the circle, Joey asked Butch very politely if he would move over a bit. Then he got down on his knees, took the steely out of his pocket, and looked towards the center of the circle. Right in the middle and not far behind the blue shooter, was a cluster of about twenty marbles. Joey hutched down and took aim.

All of a sudden, I realized what he was up to. I watched as his shooter went right for the huge blue marble and, upon impact, split the huge blue marble in two. Joey's shooter continued on through the center of the ring and smashed into the cluster of marbles. They scattered, with thirteen existing the ring. The kids started screaming "Joey! Joey! Joey!"

Mrs. Wilson then approached Butch and said, "I'm sorry, young man, but it appears that Joey is the winner."

Butch pulled out another shooter and said, "I still have one more that I can use."

"No, I'm afraid not," she said. "The rules are quite explicit: only two shooters per player. Joey is the winner."

I saw Joey standing there, a big smile on his face, knowing that he finally beat Butch. Our Principal, Mrs. Wilson, and Mrs. Hopkins presented Joey with the trophy and the savings bond.

After a tremendous applause, Joey passed the trophy around so everyone who wanted to got a chance to hold it.

Then Butch walked up to Joey, and I got there in time to hear Butch say, "You do know that if I had got to use my shooter, you would not have won."

Eddie was there too "Butch," he said, "it wasn't the shooter that won the game for Joey, it was these fifty-one marbles," and he opened his hands to show Butch.

At home that evening, it took a lot of explaining to Mom why Joey had lost his marbles in the first place. She was happy, though, when Joey gave her more than one thousand of his won marbles for her day care center.

And the trophy? The huge silver and black piece of plastic is sitting right on top of our brand new 19" black and white TV set.

About the author:

Born and raised in Vallejo, California, I graduated from Hogan Senior High School in 1964 and after a short stint as a Stevedore at Port Chicago, joined the Navy in November 1965. Following basic training in San Diego, my career started as a Communications Yeoman, being assigned to NAS Lemoore (California) and the Naval Communications Station on Guam. Upon completion of Enlisted Intelligence School, I was stationed at Keflavik, Iceland and Naples, Italy (three tours) being assigned to several NATO Staff's. Sea duty deployments included Vietnam (USS BROOKE) and the Persian Gulf (USS ANTRIM) where I served as Ship's Secretary. One noted highlight of my career was being assigned as an AFEES Test Examiner in the New York and Pennsylvania back country. Prior to retiring from the Navy in July, 1990, I completed my Associate of Arts degree in Business Administration (University of La Verne – Naples, Italy, Overseas Program)

Both during and after my Navy career, I worked as a Sous Chef at the Top of the Rock enlisted club in Keflavik, Iceland; the Rivera Fontana Blue in Naples, Italy and upon returning to the States in June, 1991, at the San Francisco Express Restaurant in Cordelia, California, located a short distance north of San Francisco. When the restaurant closed, I went to work for BART (Bay Area Rapid Transportation) where I am currently employed. Giovanna (my wife of 36 years) and I reside in Fairfield, California.

FIRE-FIGHT ON THE ROAD TO TAL-AFAR
©2012 by Donald Macnow

The morning dawned crisp and clear on the day the team left Camp Diamondback, their base in the city of Mosul. It looked to be a perfect day. A day, when back in the states, a guy might take his girlfriend to the town park, the one with a lake. They might spread out a blanket by the water's edge and dip their bare feet into the calm water and watch the ducks swim by. It should have been a day for love, not war. But it was not to be a peaceful walk in the park on this mission. The calm morning would turn out to be hot and sticky later that day, and the moisture that stained a Kevlar jacket would not be sweat, but blood.

The mission was to patrol the road to Tal-Afar, a city with a population of approximately a quarter-of-a-million people and situated in the northwestern desert near the Syrian border. The distance between Mosul and Tal-Afar is about 45 miles, an easy ride back in the states, but a hellish one in Iraq, and the trip would not be a piece of cake. There was reported insurgent activity on the eastern outskirts of the city, in a small wheat farming village, and the area had to be made secure before an US Senate fact-finding delegation made an inspection tour of the North Western sectors.

The convoy consisted of four armored Humvees, and they headed west, the rising sun behind them. The men knew the trip would be nerve-wracking and dangerous but made no mention of it. After all, they were soldiers—fearless and ready to do battle no matter what the circumstances.

Sgt. William Granger's Hummer was the second vehicle in the convoy, with Pfc. Sam Abbott and Pfc. Louis Robinson as his crew. Louis was in the turret manning the .50 caliber machine gun with Sam alongside him, binoculars hung around his neck, standing lookout. The assignments suited the two men. Louis was an excellent marksman having spent many hours hunting while on camping trips in the mountains near his home. Sam learned his skills as lookout for The Nighthawks, a street gang he belonged to back home in Detroit before joining the Army.

It was uncanny the friendship between the two men. One doesn't often see close friendships between a white redneck cracker from the rural Southwest and a black inner-city kid from a Northern ghetto. Their backgrounds were so diametrically different, but perhaps that was the catalyst for their bond. In their own way they were loners, but together they were like ebony and ivory keys on a piano: side by side in harmony with each other.

Sam would relate stories of inner city life, how he survived with the support of his "brothers" in a street gang. But even then he was a loner, a member of the gang but not really part of it, not going along with the rest of them when they mugged an old man for pocket change. Louis told of his solitary sojourns into the barren hills of Nevada and how he survived off the land shooting rabbits and cooking them over a wood fire.

In the late afternoon, when the sun was low on the horizon and blazing into their eyes, and the wind spun dirt devils across the empty fields and blew sand into their face, the convoy received a message from their HQ. A team from Fort Stark, the sniper training center stationed in Sinjar, had successfully swept the western portion of the road and had not encountered enemy opposition. They had completed their mission and were enjoying a beer in Tal-Afar. This was welcome news but it made the men complacent. They picked up the pace, anxious to get the assignment over with. Big mistake, the men lost focus. They were thinking of beer and not the insurgents, and it was disastrous.

The attack came when they were just a few miles outside of town while passing a small wheat field. Without warning an improvised explosive device (IED) disabled the first Hummer, team leader Lt. DelValle's vehicle. Fortunately, the Hummer was the M1114 model, one of the newer up-armored vehicles, and though it was out of action with the front wheels blown out, the men were unharmed.

Seconds later the sounds of rocket propelled grenades filled the air. One of the RPGs landed on the road a few feet in front of the third Hummer in the convoy sending dirt and debris into the air. Sergeant Lopez, the driver, trying to avoid the crater made by the explosive executed a violent turn to the left, and the new top-heavy style vehicle did what it often does when making violent turns: it rolled over on its side. The men were unhurt but it rendered the turret gun useless. The last Humvee received a direct hit and was completely out of action. The turret gunner and his spotter were dead, and the .50 caliber machine gun was destroyed, a scrap of twisted metal. Sergeant Granger's vehicle was the only one not damaged and operational.

The men acted instinctively and responded to the attack with a barrage of bullets into two storage buildings located in the center of the wheat field. The firepower effectively kept the insurgents inside their fortress and unable to return machine gun fire or launch RPGs.

Lt. DelValle radioed the men: "Lopez, what's your status?"

We're OK, Lieutenant, but the .50 is out of action. We rolled over and the gun is facing into the north field.

"Stevens, how bad are you hit?"

Bad, Lieutenant. I think Bill and Richie are dead. The turret is gone, totally destroyed.

"Granger, are you guys OK?"

Yes, Lieutenant, we're operational, all Ok.

"I think the RPG came from the hut on the right. I'll keep the 50 on it. The rest of you guys, except you, Granger, get the hell out of your vehicle and get into the ditch on the side of the road. Keep up the cover fire. Granger, listen up. Cut across the field and flank the western building from the left."

Granger replied: *OK, Lieutenant, roger that.*

Sgt. Granger's vehicle left the road and plowed through the wheat field towards the insurgents' building while letting loose a hail of machine gun fire into the open window. It would have been suicide for anyone to expose himself or to try and return fire while the .50 cal spewed bullets, and the Humvee would have made it to the side of the building except for another bit of bad luck.

Lt. DelValle didn't see what happened next, but in his headphones he heard Granger shouting to his men: *"Oh shit! Hold on guys, were going over!*

Sgt. Granger's Humvee was traveling over rough terrain on the narrow dirt path alongside an irrigation canal and had almost reached the insurgents' fortification, but he miscalculated the distance between his vehicle and the irrigation ditch. The right front wheel of his vehicle slipped into the water and the Hummer rolled over on its side, spilling Louis and Ben out of the turret firing station and on to the ground.

They scrambled back to the Hummer and shouted out to Sgt. Granger: *Pete, are you OK?*

Yeah, I think so, but I can't get the door open, it's jammed.

Louis replied: *Hold tight. We'll climb up and try to open it.*

Lt. DelValle cut in: "Stay put, God damn it! I can't see the side window of the west building from here. I won't be able to cover you. You guys will be cut to pieces if you try and get at the door. Make for the building and keep up the fire so they can't get to the window. Pete's going to be OK. I'm calling for help. Just keep cool you guys and do what you've been trained to do."

Instinct and training took over. Louis and Sam took turns running and covering. Sam ran towards the single room building while Louis fired full automatic at the window, and when Sam hit the dirt, Louis covered.

Within a few minutes the two men were at the redoubt, standing alongside the building, their backs up against the cement wall, a few feet from the shattered window. It was suddenly silent, and curiosity got the best of one of the insurgents. He stood up and looked out the window, preparing to fire his weapon. Louis was waiting for such an opportunity. He riddled the insurgent with bullets, tossed a grenade into the building, and then, for safety's sake, lobbed in another.

The two GIs looked at each other and smiled with relief. They hadn't any idea as to how the rest of the firefight was going but their little battle, for the moment, was over. Sam went into the building first, followed by Louis. They stepped through the window, not being mindful of broken glass because there wasn't a shard left.

The interior of the warehouse was devastated. The walls of the building were pockmarked with bullet holes. Dust filled the air, and grains of wheat stained red with blood carpeted the floor. The air smelled of cordite, making Louis think of how Robert Duval loved the smell of napalm in the movie *Apocalypse Now*.

The man Louis shot had taken the brunt of the explosion. He was shredded. There were two other men lying on the floor, dripping blood, obviously dead, their bodies crumpled like mannequins carelessly tossed to the ground, but it was not evident if the machine gun fire or the grenade took their lives. In the corner of the building lay sacks of harvested wheat. The uppermost sacks were torn and grains of wheat flowed out of the cloth like falling grains of sand in an hourglass.

Suddenly there was movement under the sacks. The black muzzle of an AK-47 slowly poked its ugly head out from under the gray cloth, and it was obvious the target would be Louis. Sam acted instinctively. He leapt forward, hands reaching for the muzzle in an attempt to divert the weapon, but he was a millisecond too late. The muzzle was diverted a few degrees, but several rounds were fired, and one of them clipped the side of Sam's head, sending his unfastened helmet soaring across the room.

Louis instinctively let loose a barrage of firepower into the wheat sacks. When the clip was empty he tore at the sacks in an uncontrollable rage, exposing the insurgent's body. He was dead, his robe stained with red, but Louis reloaded and fired until the body was unrecognizable and there was only bloody pulp instead of a face.

Louis turned his attention to Sam and knelt down beside his friend lying prostrate on the floor, his head resting on a dead insurgent's torso. The blood from the two men joined to form a stream of red. Louis shed bitter tears. There was nothing he could do; Sam was gone.

After a few minutes, the firefight raging outside stopped. The battle was over. Louis rose to his feet, but before he left the wrecked building he looked back at the combined blood of his friend and the Iraqi insurgent.

Blood is blood, Louis thought. *I can't tell Sam's from the bad guy's.*

About the author:

Borrowing a line from Forest Gump, Donald Macnow often says, "Life is like a box of chocolates, you never know what you're gonna get."

Mr. Macnow and his wife Georgianna have shared many unconventional experiences and they are reflected in his short stories. They have traveled the USA and Europe often living in campgrounds and sleeping in Army pup tents. Extended residences have been in a converted garage in the Texas dustbowl, and a house shared with farm animals in a rural German village.

After attending Hunter College his eclectic career included teaching electronics at a military training base, employment with IBM, incorporating a business machine company, an irrigation company, and the development and manufacturer of proprietary electronic tools.

Now retired, Donald Macnow indulges in his interests: tennis, sailing, sculpture, antique cars, writing, and things that go bump in the night. His soon to be published book: *The Ouija Board*

Killer weaves his experiences with the paranormal into a novel of demonic possession.

Mr. Macnow lives with his wife in Glen Cove, NY. They have two children, Scott and Laura, and six grandchildren.

LIONEL PORTWOOD
©2012 by Simone Hanson

Lionel Portwood caught the biggest fish he'd ever catch when he was fifteen years old. He got his picture in the paper, a Bluefin hanging next to him from the hook of an outsized fishing pole. Lionel was always big for his age, but still, it had been a hard haul and he had done it almost completely by himself.

Forty years later he came across that picture, so far in the past it was like looking at a stranger, or someone else's child. The bright eyes and grin took him by surprise; he remembered trying to make his face nonchalant, to make the people who might see his picture in the paper think this was something he did every day. But he saw now, as an old man, how he had failed. Even through the faded ink, it was plain to see this boy was proud.

As Lionel held the faded page in his hand, he was happy for this boy. Happy that he didn't know just how easy it really is to catch a fish, even a fighter, when you're young. Not everyone gets to have that moment, that pinprick of time when nothing is harsh and everything is an earthly miracle.

Lionel put the picture back and picked up the photo album he had originally set out to find. Before he could open it he held it against his chest, hugging it like a child, as though he wanted to console it; or, perhaps, find some consolation for himself. He felt older than his fifty-five years, the events of the past few days falling down hard on him. He was shattered. And he knew that even when he fitted himself back together, he'd remain fragile.

Nothing in his life had been portentous, rather more like something *Farmers' Almanac* would predict for a local boy. He'd married young, had a family and, in the tradition of Maine fishing families, he'd gradually taken over his father's lobster boat and territory. His wife, Beverly, ran the lobster pound, and over the years had created a veritable seafood heaven. The Portland paper had even done a story on her, claiming that if the Legislature ever got around to naming a State Lobster Pound, it would be Portwood's All Things Fishy. Lionel had framed the article, which included a picture of Beverly, in a thin black frame with off-white matting right after it appeared in the paper. He hung it over the counter of the shop without telling her, and she didn't notice until a customer pointed it out and congratulated her. She turned to look at it and was struck by how imposing and important it seemed to be, this story about her and Lionel. It would be a few years before the familiarity of the framed article would cause it to fade from her mind and the only time she'd really notice it was when it got dusty and needed to be cleaned.

Their first child was a girl, Estelle, who grew up fast and healthy, and fit neatly into the lifestyle of two people who outpaced the sun every morning, worked a hard day and didn't rest until the boat was secured and the floor of the shop was bleached free of the briny drippings of the lobster, crab and shrimp brought into the pound six days a week.

The second child was a boy, and the day he was born, Lionel felt that he'd reached some type of plateau, like he could stop climbing for a while. And so Beverly and Lionel settled onto the flat plane of their lives together, and that was it. Gathering lobsters in crippling cold and withstanding the competition of inferior, but cheaper, supermarket specials were the challenges they were prepared for, the stationary life they had worked so hard to embrace.

And it was fine. It was fine except when Lionel caught a tourist eyeing his daughter or striking up a conversation with his son. On those occasions, he thought his family was being made part of the tourist experience, what visitors hoped to see on their Maine getaway.

In those moments, he saw his family as they did. Estelle was plain, even in his eyes. There was nothing in her looks that was unattractive, but she had no features that could be called pretty. It was almost, he thought sometimes, a remarkable feat of nature that a girl could be without a single trace of beauty. A stunning compilation of ordinariness that made her almost invisible. But she had a presence, Lionel knew, a certain way of carrying herself, of talking to people, that put them at ease. She was the reason their customers kept coming back, her dry humor making them laugh, her deference making them feel important. They just never noticed.

George, his son, could haul a lobster trap like it was a child's beach bucket, and at the end of the day could drink his weight in beer and still carry himself home. And Lionel was proud of this brand of masculinity and all that George was capable of, and yet when these people from away would talk and coax lobstermen stories out of him, Lionel would tremble.

They wouldn't know the strength of will it took to live this life. How could they? Where would that fair-weather man get the strength and patience to untangle trap lines? What about the wherewithal it took to head a boat straight into a wave when the instinct is to turn away from it? Those flatlanders had more in common with ballerinas than the stock George came from.

"So, what's the word on the high seas?" one of the customers would ask.

"Well," George would start, "they're makin' us use this new sink rope now."

"Sink rope? I haven't heard of it."

In his quiet voice that rose and fell like gentle waves, dropping and adding r's as only a real Mainer can do, he'd answer them, believing he was educating them in something that was important, because it was important to *him*.

"Sink rope, something the darn legislature has come up with. Seems like they got nothing better to do but cost us money.

Supposed to save the whales. But I don't know, ain't never seen a whale out in these waters, have I?"

Lionel would scratch the back of his neck, trying to loosen the tension. George was just so damn honest, there he'd go, talking all day to whoever had a mind to listen, even if they listened with a pale smile on their faces, nodding their heads at him like they were all in this together. And George, slapping them on their L.L. Bean backs, telling them to be sure and come back before they left for home.

"Nice people," he'd always say when they'd driven away, heading back to their rented cottages as he headed back to the boat.

But Lionel knew, somewhere in the back of his mind, that they meant well, the tourists and the summer people. They could have bought everything they needed at the supermarket, but they wanted to support the locals, to help maintain the way of life they admired and wished they could be a part of. They liked the experience of it all, being part of that chain of events; part of the process of facing the ocean every day, transporting the catch to trucks, then tanks and coolers, and finally wrapping it up in the local newspaper, and loading their dinners into the trunks of their cars.

If he thought about it, he'd have to admit they did make this way of life possible. It's just that it bothered him a little that the piece they took out of his life was a vacation for them, nothing real. Just a story they'd tell when they got home.

He didn't mind so much for himself, but it mattered when it came to his children. He'd watch the New York parents swing their angel child between them, bags of lobster and Beverly's crab cakes in their free hands, their private words sounding like songs.

The music of Lionel's world was an orchestra of heavy diesel engines and screaming seagulls that circled his boat as soon as the bait bags were opened, growing in numbers so large they cast shadows over the deck. And George had wanted to be a member of this ensemble as soon as he was old enough to be aware of its existence. Lionel had started him out filling bait bags, and gradually let him measure the lobsters as they were pulled out of the traps, slowing the whole process down just so he could get the feel of a live lobster. But Lionel didn't care, and he had such a way of looking at George as he measured each lobster, his crew knew to keep quiet about it.

When George was seventeen, Lionel let him start hauling. When he was eighteen, there was no difference between George and the guys who worked the boat. He could band a lobster faster than anyone in history and he learned the careful art of curbing his enthusiasm at a large catch, recognizing that fishing is hard work not a sport.

When George could squint his eyes at a thousand-pound catch and say, "That's reasonable," Lionel knew his son was one of them—except his penchant for throwing the last of the bait to the waiting gulls because he hated that they spent all day flying on hope. Lionel would shake his head and tell him he was all but begging those gulls to follow them around every day.

"There's no harm in it," George would say. "And anyway, it's good luck."

Lionel would shake his head again and tell him when he was done playing King Neptune of the Sea, he could meet him at the Fishnet. But he'd always wait for him anyway, watching until George had rinsed his gloves and thrown them into the wheelhouse.

At twenty-one, George married the town wallflower, so drunk with happiness his parents could only look at each other and hope for the best. "Let him alone," Lionel had told his wife. "He knows what he's doing. He's a man now." She had smiled her agreement, because what else could they do? And yet, as the couple walked down the aisle of the church, Lionel thought the young wife clutched his arm with more desperation than ardor. And when he noticed that George had accidentally tucked his pant leg into the back of his sock, it broke his heart a little.

And then George was on his own. Lionel had reached the point where he saw his son as a finished piece, feeling like a metal smith who has finally turned off the torch and scrutinizes his work. And George was a fine piece, hardworking and honest. And that's what it took to get along in this world, in this kind of life. Lionel had done right by him, he knew. And he did not expect to have to turn around at any point in his life, least of all when he was old and less able to bear weight, and worry that he had done nothing more than make a series of mistakes.

As Lionel stood there, on what happened to be a dark and cold afternoon, in the dim light of the den, he put down the photograph of himself, and he held the book of pictures close to him, afraid to open it up. Afraid to look at pictures of George and see a different boy, because by now, it would be too late. *Rectify*. The word was in his head, and his head was a hall of mirrors, reflecting the word over and over, infinitely.

Three days before, George had been heading toward the boat, Lionel and their crew following right behind him, the dock undulating beneath them because the wind was up and the waves were short and choppy. It wasn't snowing, just a sharp, cutting chill. Lionel didn't want to admit to George that it might be a little too cold and rough out there, that maybe they should leave it for the day. But the visibility was good, so he said nothing. It was always possible to turn around and come back, so he hunched his shoulders together and lowered his head so his face wouldn't take the brunt of the wind. For the first time, he noticed that George walked the same way in the cold.

A strong, sudden gust caught Lionel's cap. It almost felt like a kid grabbing it off his head and throwing it into the water, like some kind of joke.

"I got it, Dad."

"Leave it, George. I got the woolen one in the boat. Freeze my ears off, I wear that one."

But George was on his knees already, one hand on a metal tie-down, the other reaching for the baseball cap, which inched away from the dock, and then inched back, making it impossible to tell whether it was within reach or not.

Lionel said it again. "Leave it. I don't need it." He remembered the words, remembered the sound they made, discernable even as George tipped beyond the balancing point. He landed in the water silently, all sound lost in the slapping of the waves and the wail of the wind.

George's waders were bright orange and they filled with water quickly, and the weight of the water pulled him down. Lionel was screaming; yes he was, this quiet man who embraced his life as a respected foe, too reverential—until now—to curse and scream. He lay prostrate on the dock, reaching for his son, grabbing the suspenders as he went under, screaming to his friends to help him, to help him pull.

Thirty seconds is about all a person has in frigid November waters, and it took at least five minutes to pull George back onto the dock. Lionel blew into his mouth, pounded his chest, ordered him to get up, but George lay still. Lionel took off his jacket and covered his son, but George stayed cold, even when Lionel lay on top of him.

All he had left now were the pictures, the ones he held in his arms, bound in a closed book. Lionel breathed slowly as he set the book down on his desk, and his hands fumbled slightly as he opened it. His eyes took a moment to register the images before him, unfamiliar at first glance, until he saw George in each frame. Formal baby pictures with his sister. Here he was with a fishing pole, no fish, but at least a pole. Missing teeth. A shepherd in the Christmas pageant. Holding a lobster with no bands on it. Tossing a graduation cap. His wedding. Lionel pulled away the plastic sheeting, tore them off the sticky cardstock paper, fell to his knees as he dropped them to the floor. He tried to hold them all at once, these pictures of his son, smiling—laughing even—all his life.

About the author:

Simone Hanson lives in Roswell, Georgia with her husband, three boys, two dogs, and one kitten. She is a former school administrator and lawyer but left the working world to stay home with her children because she is not the supermom she thought she was going to be. She has been working on the same novel for years now, and occasionally needs to take a break from it and write a short story. 'Lionel Portwood' is one of those short stories. Originally from Maine, her writing is set there as it is the place she knows and loves the best.

She is thrilled to have a second short story selected by Scribes Valley Publishing.

www.ingramcontent.com/pod-product-compliance
Lightning Source LLC
Chambersburg PA
CBHW051309170626
46809CB00004B/1824